LITTLE BROTHER

PATRIOT KIDS OF THE AMERICAN REVOLUTION SERIES BOOK 4

GEOFF BAGGETT

Cocked Hat
Publishing

DEDICATION

For Jacob Henry Martin, my grandson and proud member of the Sons of the American Revolution. I cannot wait to get him into his first living history uniform.

Cover Design by Natasha Snow - natashasnow.com

PART I

ONE BRAVE BOY - 1776

DOMINOES AND REBELLION

April 20, 1776
Saturday Evening – Guilford Courthouse, North Carolina

The night was soft and quiet, and uncharacteristically cool for late April, even in the Carolina Piedmont. Almost every chimney in the town belched a steady stream of gray-white smoke. The heavy, humid air caused most of the smoke to remain low in the atmosphere and hover like a hazy blanket above the rooftops of the sleepy little North Carolina village of Guilford Courthouse. No one wandered the streets after dark. It was a Saturday evening. Most respectable people in the township had already retired to the privacy of their homes.

The typical sounds of village life emanated from those homes. There was a mixture of piano music, singing, muffled laughter, and the occasional crying baby. In the distance, several annoying dogs barked. On the northern side of town, a very misinformed and confused rooster crowed. The freshly plowed fields and pastures beyond the edges of the township were dark and silent. It was a soft, quiet night, indeed.

Like most of the other simple, whitewashed frame houses along Main Street in Guilford Courthouse, an orange-yellow flicker of fire and candlelight escaped through the milky glass windows of the James Billingsley home. The dancing light bathed the tiny lawn and gardens beyond with a soft glow. Very few sounds came from the Billingsley abode. Six of the family's nine children were gone from home. They were all married and managing houses and families of their own. Only the youngest three children remained in their father's house: fifteen-year-old Martha, fourteen-year-old Walter, and the little brother of the family, Basil, age eleven.

The sun had been below the horizon for almost an hour, and it would soon be time for bed. James, the father and master of the home, preferred going to bed early and rising early. Even though he had surrendered his farm to his older sons and purchased a house in town several years ago, Mr. Billingsley still preferred to keep "farmer's hours" in his daily life.

The Billingsley family always retired early on Saturday evenings, since Sunday was Mr. Billingsley's primary work day. He was a preacher, and he served in several small Baptist congregations throughout the region. On most Sundays, James preached at least three sermons in the nearby Sandy Creek and Abbots Creek Baptist Churches. He was a passionate, fiery, energetic preacher. So, going to bed early on a Saturday night was something of a necessity. He needed the extra rest to carry him through his exhausting work the following day.

It was a wonder that the man was not already snoozing

in his comfy feather bed. On this particular night, however, he was simply too absorbed in poring over the pages of the latest *Virginia Gazette*, a newspaper published in faraway Williamsburg. He sat in his favorite rocking chair beside the front window, nursing a cup of warm milk flavored with nutmeg, and enjoying his weekly paper. He had been quite animated in his reading that evening, occasionally slapping his hand on his knee and proclaiming an enthusiastic, "Amen!"

The other members of the family were all gathered in the parlor for the evening, as well. In addition to the large, crackling fire in the fireplace, approximately two dozen beeswax candles adorned stands throughout the room, providing ample light for all who were gathered there. The fragrant candles filled the entire room with the pleasant, sweet smell of honey.

Though they were all gathered in the same room, James' wife and children each devoted their attentions to their unique endeavors and interests. Tomorrow was Sunday. There would be no idle leisure activities, chores, or games on the Sabbath. Such things were not allowed. As usual, Sunday would be a day filled with church services, Scripture readings, seriousness, and prayer. The members of the Billingsley clan intended to reap at least one more hour of happy entertainment from this pleasant Saturday evening before their father ordered them all to bed.

Mrs. Elizabeth Billingsley sat opposite her husband in a rocking chair that was identical to his. She sipped a cup of spiced milk, as well. She busied herself by mending several sets of wool stockings afflicted with ripped, hole-infested toes. It was a very familiar weekly task in this faithful mother's life. Raising six boisterous boys had always provided her with an endless flow of torn, shredded items of clothing in need of repair.

The elegant young maiden, Martha, sat quietly in a comfortable, padded Queen Anne chair in the far corner of the room. Like her father, she, too, was reading. However, she did not care for the newspapers and political pamphlets that her father liked to read. Instead, she was enjoying, for at least the third time, the thrilling words of Jonathan Swift's adventurous novel, *Gulliver's Travels.*

Walter and Basil, the youngest of the six Billingsley boys, lay on their bellies on the floor in front of the fireplace. Each had a soft goose feather pillow tucked beneath his chest and chin. They were engaged in a fiercely competitive contest of dominoes. It was only a matter of time before some explosion of conflict between the two boys would bring an end to the tranquility of this otherwise peaceful Saturday evening. It had happened far too many times before.

The sharp click of an ivory chip being deposited in victory ended the Billingsley silence and peace.

"And that, Basil, is the final play. We have reached a stalemate. Once again, I am the victor."

"No, Walter! You did not win!" squealed Basil, rising to his knees. "You have more dominoes left over than I do!" The headstrong, competitive nine-year-old was angry. He was on the edge of livid, actually. Basil despised losing, especially to Walter.

Their father lowered his newspaper ever so slightly and glared at them over the top of his spectacles. He considered saying something, but decided that, thus far, the developing conflict had not risen to the level of fatherly intervention. The boys' mother sighed in frustration. She knew that an explosion of anger was imminent. Margaret rolled her eyes with an air of drama that only a teen-aged sister could muster.

Walter, five years Basil's elder, maintained a calm demeanor, but rejoiced on the inside. He, too, anticipated that a juvenile fit would soon visit the Billingsley household. He knew better than anyone the simple, yet effective methods required to trigger an emotional explosion out of his younger brother. He loved to watch Basil throw a temper tantrum and then get into trouble with his parents afterwards. The corners of Walter's mouth curved upward, forming a wry, mischievous grin.

"Now, Little Brother, if you will simply recall the rules of the game, you will realize that I am, as usual, the winner. Once again, I remind you that it is not the number of dominoes in hand that determines the victor. It is the number of pips on the game pieces. The fewest pips wins. My three dominoes have a total of seven pips. Your two dominoes have a combined total of nine. Therefore, I win the game."

Basil growled. He hated being called, "Little Brother." Yet, everyone in his family insisted on doing just that. Walter knew that he hated it ... that is exactly why he said it. Walter grinned and waited anxiously for Basil to explode.

On the far side of the room Margaret giggled quietly. Basil's ears turned red in embarrassment when he realized that his brother was correct. The veins on his forehead throbbed. His hands began to tremble. He clenched his fists, preparing to fight.

He exploded in anger and frustration, "Cheater!"

Basil jumped to his feet and kicked viciously at the dominoes that stretched in a long line on the wide pine floorboard in front of the fireplace. Several of the ivory game pieces launched dangerously close to the flames.

Walter screeched, "You annoying little toad!" He dived to retrieve his precious dominoes from the scorching fire.

James Billingsley could no longer tolerate the conflict between his sons.

"Boys! Stop it this instant! I will not have the two of you ruining the waning moments of this glorious day with your selfish bitterness and callous words. Walter, you will cease referring to your brother in such unkind terms. And Basil, you must learn now to control that temper of yours. If you find yourself unable to remember the rules of the game, you should stop playing it." He shook his newspaper in disgust. "I grow weary of this insufferable bickering between the two of you that invades our home almost every evening. I will not stand for it anymore. Do you understand?"

"Yes, Father," answered Walter firmly.

"Yes, Father," echoed Basil. His trembling voice was barely above a whisper.

"Very well, then." James paused and took a deep, cleansing breath. "Now, I want you all to gather 'round. Put away your games and books. I must tell you about the latest developments at our Fourth Provincial North Carolina Congress."

"Oh, Father!" wailed Martha, rolling her eyes again. She rolled her eyes a lot. "Must we suffer more of your boring politics?"

"My dear daughter, the events of recent days in this colony go far beyond politics as usual," responded James. "Now come closer, all of you. You must hear this!"

His sons and daughter reluctantly but obediently crossed the room and joined their parents. Walter politely fetched a small stool for his sister. The boys, as was their custom, sat cross-legged in the floor at their father's feet.

Mr. Billingsley declared, "I believe that we are on the

cusp of a rebellion against England that will soon sweep across this continent and forever change the face of the Americas. Surely, it will be our American Revolution!"

His wife emitted a loud sigh and frustratingly dropped the stocking that she had been mending into her lap. She almost glared at her husband.

"Darling, surely you do not believe that the horrible rebellion in Boston will reach us way down here in the South. We are at peace in North Carolina."

James stared sternly at his wife. His voice dropped in tone, sounding almost like a growl. "Do not make light of the sacrifices of our Patriots in the North, my dear. Many have shed their blood and given their lives in response to the tyranny of King George III. And contrary to your claim, I submit to you that we are not at peace. Rebellion is coming to the Carolinas. I am certain of it."

"But why would we wish to rebel against England now?" moaned Elizabeth. "King George does not bother us out here on the frontier. The farming is successful and pays well. Our economy is good. Lately, the troublesome Indians have been staying on their side of the mountains."

"And yet, many of our friends have fled over those distant mountains in search of freedom, and to escape King George's back-breaking taxes." He paused dramatically. His eyes widened with excitement. "And I, too, feel tempted to follow them in search of that same freedom."

"James!" his wife scolded him in disbelief. "Surely, you would not simply walk away from our precious lands and our other financial holdings." She waved her hand in a wide circle, dramatically highlighting the expanse of their majestic house. "How could you ever leave this beautiful, stately home less than one block from our county courthouse? James, you are revered and respected in this county. This is our home!"

"Are we going to move over the mountains, Papa?" interrupted Basil excitedly. He rattled off a barrage of eager questions. "Can we live in a log cabin? Can I wear buckskin breeches? Do we have to speak Cherokee? I would love to see a real bear!"

James sighed at his son and patted him on his head. "No, Basil, we are not moving over the mountains." He turned to his wife. "But perhaps I would go, Elizabeth, if I thought that I might have the opportunity to find liberty and breathe air that is truly free."

"God forbid the notion!" she retorted.

Her children gasped. They had never before heard their mother issue such a scandalous swear.

This time Elizabeth's voice emanated from her tiny, quivering lips in the form of a growl. "I will not leave my home and my grown sons and daughters. And I will not miss out on seeing my grandchildren grow up, just so that you can go in search of your strange notion of freedom."

James smiled victoriously. "Most likely, we will not be required to leave our home, my love. It seems that freedom is attempting to find its way to us."

"Whatever do you mean?" she asked, confused.

He shook his newspaper victoriously. "The Fourth Provincial North Carolina Congress just closed its session in Halifax last week. They authorized our representatives to the Continental Congress in Philadelphia to cast their votes for independence from Great Britain!"

"What?" his wife responded in disbelief.

"What does that mean, Papa?" asked Walter curiously.

James beamed with pride and held up the newspaper. "It means that, if the Continental Congress ever considers a declaration of independence from Great Britain, the North Carolina men can vote to separate. The text of their decision is here in the *Gazette*. Listen to what those brave, noble men declared ..." He cleared his throat and began reading.

"*Since all sincere efforts for justice by the United Colonies have been ignored or rejected by out mother nation and King, this committee recommends that this body of representatives adopt the following resolution: The delegates for this Colony in the Continental Congress are hereby empowered to concur with the other delegates of the other Colonies in declaring Independence from Great Britain.*"

He stopped reading, and then added, "The vote on this resolve was unanimous. Eighty-three voted for it. None in the assembly voted against it."

The Billingsley family sat in stunned silence. Even the aloof Margaret seemed captivated by the notion of an outright rebellion against England. Basil did not understand a single word that his father had just read, but he knew that it all sounded very important.

"Will there be a shooting war in North Carolina, Papa?" asked Margaret. "Here amongst our fields and homes?"

James drew in a deep breath. "Perhaps one day there will, Margaret. Some of your brothers may even be called upon to serve the causes of freedom and liberty."

Walter declared, "I will fight, Papa. I want to fight for freedom! I want to go with my brothers!" He held his chin high and poked out his chest in pride and defiance.

"Me, too, Papa!" echoed Basil, not willing to be outdone by his older brother.

James grinned at his sons and tousled their hair. "Do not worry yourselves any further regarding fighting and wars on this peaceful night. We will simply have to wait and see what our future holds in store for us." James rose to his feet.

"Now ... off to bed, all of you. We will discuss these matters on another day."

The children all rose obediently, kissed their mother and father, and then ascended the stairs to their bedchambers. James and Elizabeth watched them lovingly and proudly. Moments later the doors to their rooms clicked shut as each of them prepared for bed.

RUN FOR HELP!

2:00 AM – That Same Night

Walter bolted awake. He lay flat on his back and remained perfectly still in his bed. Something had roused him from a deep sleep. But what was it?

As he fought to overcome the disorientation of sleep and the haunting darkness of the night, he realized that it was some sort of sound that had awakened him. It was a strange sound ... deep, booming, and loud. He was unsure about its source. All he knew was that the sound was out of place. It was wrong, somehow. It was not a sound that one would expect to hear in the wee hours of the morning on a Sunday.

Walter was relatively certain that the noise had its origins from somewhere outside the house. Several dogs roused throughout the neighborhood, unleashing an annoying and expanding chorus of barks and howls. That, too, was odd for the middle of the night.

Suddenly, he heard the sound again. This time he knew

what it was. It was a fist pounding on the front door of his home.

"What in heaven's name?" he muttered angrily. "Who would call at such an indecent hour?"

On the other side of the bedchamber he heard Basil's bed creak. He glanced toward the place where his little brother slept. The fireplace beyond contained only a remnant of embers from the evening fire. In the dull glow of the dusky orange coals, Walter could see Basil sitting up in his bed. The boy was grinding both of his fists into his tired eyes.

Basil groaned, "What was that sound, Walter? Was it thunder?"

"No. Someone is knocking on our door. I heard it twice."

"In the middle of the night?" whined Basil. "It must be something bad. Maybe someone has died and they have come to fetch Papa."

"Not likely. Those kinds of things usually wait until morning. No one makes funeral or burial plans in the middle of the night."

"Well, what is it, then?"

Walter shook his head in the darkness. "I do not know, but I am going to find out."

Walter threw back his blankets and walked toward the fireplace. He grabbed a handful of tinder from a basket on the mantle and tossed it onto the glowing coals. He leaned over and blew vigorously on the dry material, which immediately burst into lively, bright flames. He took a sterling silver three-candle stand from the mantle, removed a short beeswax candle, and lit the charred wick in the fresh flames. He used that candle to light the other two on the stand.

As he turned and began walking away from the fireplace, once again a fist slammed against the downstairs outer door. There were three thunderous knocks. Both boys jumped at the sound. This time the banging was accompanied by a loud, harsh voice.

"James Billingsley! I demand that you open this door! By the authority of King George III of Great Britain, I demand that you reveal yourself and submit to questioning!"

They heard their father's voice bellow from somewhere downstairs, "One moment, Sir! Allow a man the time to put on his breeches, for Goodness sake!"

Walter began running. Basil threw off his bedcovers and, following Walter, raced toward their chamber door. Walter opened it and both boys dashed into the upstairs hallway. They leapt down the first short flight of stairs to a small landing. Their wool stockings slid across the shiny, polished wood of the landing and they collided in a heap against the far wall. One of the candles tumbled from Walter's stand and fell to the floor, splashing a puddle of melted wax onto the floorboards. Walter quickly grabbed the candle, re-ignited its flame, and stuck it back into the stand.

Their father's stern voice rumbled from the darkness below. "Boys, stay upstairs. Go back to bed." He sounded gruff. He sounded frightened.

James Billingsley was standing alone in the darkness, behind the bolted and locked door. He was wearing black breeches and stockings. His white nightshirt hung untucked over the top of the breeches. He was not wearing any shoes.

Their father growled, "I mean it, boys. Stay upstairs."

"But, Father!" groaned Walter.

"Do not argue with me, Son! Simply do as I say!"

"Yes, Father," responded Walter.

He tugged at Basil's nightshirt and led him back up the

stairs. Once they were out of their father's line of sight, Walter blew out his candles and dropped down to the floor. He had just enough angle to see down the stairway and spy on the events below. Basil followed his brother's lead.

Basil whispered, "What are we doing, Walter?"

"Shh!" Walter held his finger over his lips, forming the universal sign of silence.

The pounding on the door resumed. The flickering light of several torches invaded the entry hall through the thick glass that adorned each side of the door. In the eerie glow of the torchlight, Walter could see the heavy wood vibrating from each blow. The invisible voice bellowed from beyond, "Open this door, in the name of King George!"

Elizabeth Billingsley peeked from behind the doorway to the parlor. She carried a single candle on a small brass stand. The boys' mother wore a heavy linen robe over the top of her shift. Her hair hung loosely over her shoulders. Walter chuckled a bit under his breath. He could not recall the last time that he had seen his mother's hair loose and not under the concealment of a bonnet.

Elizabeth whispered, "What is going on, James? What do these men want?"

"I do not know, Elizabeth. Please, darling, go back to bed. The voice does not sound like a friendly one."

"I will not return to bed! Not until I know what matter is so urgent that it requires our being roused from sleep in the middle of the night!"

James sighed frustratingly at his wife's disobedience. He composed himself as best he could, stood up straight, and tried to appear as respectable as possible in his half-dressed state. He poked out his chest with all of the pride and dignity that he could muster, and then reached out and released the locking latch on the door.

Whoever stood on the other side of that door took immediate advantage of the opening. The huge portal of thick oak exploded inward, knocking James off of his feet. Elizabeth screamed in fear. James landed with a loud thud and a cry of pain. He skidded awkwardly on his backside across the slick, polished floor. He did not stop until his head slammed into the staircase handrail.

A stocky young man of average height stepped through the door. He was wearing a huge, dark cloak. An elegant black cocked hat decorated his head. Six more men followed closely behind him. Three of them held torches. All of them were carrying British Army Brown Bess muskets. The men scattered left and right as they began a search of the bottom floor of the house.

"Be sure to search the basement thoroughly!" ordered the leader of the group.

Near the top of the stairs Basil attempted to rise to his feet. He instinctively wanted to run downstairs and protect his parents. Walter grabbed him by the arm.

"Wait!" whispered Walter.

"But, Mama and Papa need us!" protested Basil.

"There's nothing we can do against all of those soldiers." Walter paused and considered their dilemma. He quickly formulated a plan. "Basil, go to our room and get your clothes and shoes on. Slip out the back window and run to the farm and wake up our brothers. Tell them to bring men and weapons. Tell them that soldiers carrying torches and guns have come for Papa." He paused. "And tell them that Papa has been injured."

Basil stared in disbelief at his brother. "You want me to run all the way to the farm? It is over a mile outside of town!"

"Then you had better get going immediately. I will stay

here and see if I can figure something out to help Mama and Papa. Now go, Basil! Bring back James, John, Samuel, and Henry! This is bad. Really bad."

Basil started to protest Walter's instructions, but then he recognized the fear in his older brother's eyes.

He nodded reluctantly. "You can count on me, Walter. I will go as fast as I can!"

Basil turned and crawled quietly into their room. Once inside, he jumped to his feet and scurried to the pegboard that hung beside the fireplace. The clothes that he had worn the previous evening were dangling from the wooden pegs. He grabbed his stockings and shirt and plopped down on the stone hearth. He allowed the glowing coals to warm his feet and stockings as he pulled them up high over his knees.

He donned his shirt quickly, then jumped up and grabbed his wool breeches from their peg. He leaned back onto his bed and pulled the baggy pants over his feet as quickly as he could. He did not bother with his weskit and all of its annoying buttons. There was not enough time. Instead, he fetched his heavy wool overcoat as he slipped his black leather shoes onto his feet. He grabbed his hat as he darted toward the window.

Basil already had a plan in his mind. He would climb out onto the roof of the back porch, dangle from the edge, and then simply drop onto the woodpile beside the back door. It all sounded very easy. But could he actually do it?

The window proved to be his first obstacle. It refused to budge. The bedroom window had not been opened since the previous autumn. The rains and snows of winter had swollen the wood and sealed it shut. It took several seconds of shaking and pushing, but at long last the wood gave way to Basil's efforts. He raised the lower pane, opening the window just enough for him to squeeze through the narrow gap. He tossed his hat out onto the roof and then crawled out. He quickly, silently closed the window behind him.

Loud, frightening voices boomed from the front lawn. Then came angry, muffled shouts from inside the house. Basil was terrified. He crawled over the cracked, rough wooden shingles toward the edge of the porch roof and peeked over. The woodpile was several feet to his right. He shifted in that direction and prepared to jump. But he was afraid. He was more than afraid. He was terrified, actually. Basil had never been on a roof before.

The youngest Billingsley had been afraid of heights his entire life. His brothers had often teased him because of it. Despite the chiding of his brothers, he always refused to slide down the rope from the barn loft. He did not climb trees. And he would never consent to climbing a ladder to work on a roof.

As Basil peered over the edge of the shingles at the woodpile far below, he could scarcely believe that he was considering leaping from the relative safety of the rooftop.

"*Don't be a coward, Basil Billingsley!*" he scolded himself. "*You're not really going to jump, you're going to drop. Now, get moving!*"

He spun around and eased his legs over the edge. Slowly, carefully he pushed his body over the side. It did not require much effort. Gravity was already pulling him downward. He clung, terrified, to the splintery shingles. He clawed at them with his fingernails in an effort to maintain his grip on the wood.

Basil began to cry. "*I cannot do it!*" he thought. "*I cannot let go!*" He trembled with a mixture of fear and anger. He was angry at the men who had invaded his home. He was angry at Walter for making him go. And he was angry at himself for being so afraid.

Suddenly, a huge crashing sound exploded inside the dining room. Glass shattered. Basil heard his mother's wailing cry.

Basil stopped thinking about his fears. His anger at the men who were destroying his home and terrorizing his family quickly outweighed those fears.

"*These soldiers are hurting my family! I must save them!*" Basil exclaimed silently.

He released the grip of his fingers. His body floated for just a moment, then dropped quickly toward the ground below. Basil grabbed at anything that might help break his fall. His hands waved wildly and silently in the air, but there was nothing within reach.

His fall came to a sudden stop when the leather soles of his shoes landed on the four-foot-tall stack of oak and hickory firewood. Basil grunted with a mixture of surprise and pain. The shock of the sudden stop vibrated the bones in his legs and hips. His jaw suddenly slammed shut, clamping down on his tender tongue. Basil choked back a cry of pain. He tasted blood in his mouth from his ruptured tongue. He fell backward from the woodpile and landed with a hollow thud on the hard-packed earth.

Several of the logs tumbled from the pile and landed around him. One log landed across his shins, sending a wave of pain through his legs. Basil resisted his urge to scream.

A gruff voice echoed from inside the house, "What was that noise? I heard something outside! Private Jenkins, go around back immediately and see if anyone is lurking about!"

A deep, throaty voice responded, "Yes, sir!"

Moments later, Basil heard boots stomping across the boards of the front porch. Soon he saw the light of a torch bobbing in the trees to his right. Someone was coming from the front yard! It was one of the soldiers!

Basil realized that he only had a few seconds to make his escape. He ignored the pain in his tongue, hips, and legs. He rolled over onto his belly, scrambled to his feet, and ran as fast as he could toward the trees beside the barn. He had to reach the concealment of the forest before the soldier found him!

Basil ran as fast as he possibly could. He glanced fearfully over his shoulder. Just as he entered the tree line, he saw the glowing head of the flaming torch come around the corner of the house. He dived behind a large tree and lay perfectly still. He tried to control his breathing, but he was too excited. He was almost certain that the soldier could hear his loud, wheezing breath.

After a few seconds, Basil dared to peek around the edge of the tree. He was horrified by what he saw. The man was standing beside the woodpile and staring at the scattered logs. The tall fellow held his torch high in the air and scanned the area around him. Finally, after several agonizing seconds, he lowered the torch and continued walking around the house. He soon disappeared around the other corner of the building. Once the light of his torch was gone, the area plunged, once again, into the deep darkness of night.

More screaming erupted from inside the house. Basil recognized a different voice. It was his sister, Martha. The poor girl wailed hysterically. There was shouting, and then more sounds of shattering glass. A man's voice suddenly uttered vile, hideous curses.

Basil, trembling in fear and with tears streaming down

his face, took a deep breath. He rose to his feet, pulled his hat down tight onto his head, and then took off running through the woods in the direction of the Billingsley farm. He had to awaken his brothers! He had to save his family!

3

BASIL'S BATTLE

Branches slashed at Basil's face. The low-hanging, leafless limbs were impossible to see in the moonless night. Still, he pushed onward.

Shortly after disappearing into the dense woods behind his house, Basil had turned left in an effort to find his way back toward the road that led to the family farm. He simply had to find that road! He knew that he had to move quickly. His family was in grave trouble. He had to find the road soon, or risk spending the remainder of the night lost in the woods. He ran for several minutes, and quickly became frustrated.

His growing fear did not make his quest to locate the road any easier. He wondered if there were other men hiding in the woods. Horrifying thoughts filled his mind. What if he were captured? What if the men started shooting? What if he got lost and never found the road?

The idea of being lost in the woods frightened Basil the most. He had been lost in the forest near the family farm only once before. It was two summers ago, when he was only seven years old. And that was in the daytime. He remembered the sheer terror of not knowing where he was. He also remembered the joyful moment when his brother, Samuel, had finally found him. Since then, he had refused to go into the woods alone.

Yet, here he was, in the pitch black of night, running through a forest shrouded in darkness and shadows. Every tree looked like a fearsome giant. Every wisp of cold fog looked like a horrifying ghost. Basil was terrified, yet he continued onward in search of the elusive road.

"*Where is it?*" he thought. "*Where is the highway? Am I lost? Am I going the wrong way? Will I ever reach the farm?*"

Suddenly, Basil's right foot dropped into a deep hole in the forest floor. He stumbled and fell face-first onto the cold, musty ground. The dry, crunchy leaves invaded his mouth and nostrils. He quickly rose to his knees, coughing and spitting the earthy leaves from his mouth. His head throbbed from the impact with the ground. Basil wanted to just sit there and cry. He was sleepy, sore, and frightened. He did not want to run, anymore. He wished that he was back under the warm covers of his soft bed.

"*You have to keep moving!*" he scolded himself. "*Stop your whining! Your family is depending on you! Do not be such a coward!*"

Capturing a fresh surge of courage, Basil grabbed a nearby sapling and pulled himself to his feet. He slowly climbed out of the hole and then continued on his way. Minutes later he emerged from the darkness of the trees into a narrow, open gap. He looked left and right. The gap in the forest continued in both directions. He knelt down and felt the ground. It was dry and dusty.

"It's the road!" he exclaimed out loud. "I made it!"

Basil's heart thumped excitedly. He turned to his right

and ran toward the west. The Billingsley farm was less than a mile away. Though his body still ached from the fall, discovering the road had renewed his spirits. He knew that his brothers would know what to do to help Mama, Papa, Walter, and Martha. He kicked his legs and pumped his arms and ran faster than he had ever run before! He ran so hard that his lungs ached and his hands shook.

He could scarcely believe it when he rounded a bend in the road and saw the familiar entrance to the Billingsley farm. He was amazed he had covered so much ground so quickly. He thought that it would take much longer to run a whole mile! But, still, he was very tired and thirsty. His lungs wheezed, aching for air. His mouth and nose were parched.

Ahead and to his right he could see the outline of the original Billingsley farmhouse in the pale starlight. His older brother, James, and wife, Ann, lived in the old family home. Another brother, Samuel, lived in a newer house just a few hundred yards down the narrow dirt road that led deeper into the small valley.

Basil began emitting a dry, empty scream the moment that he could see the first house. His lips formed the word "James," but there was no sound.

At least a half-dozen dogs detected Basil running toward the house and unleashed a barking frenzy. Still, there was no light or movement inside. Basil began to sob out of frustration. He continued to attempt to call out his brother's name, but to no avail. At last, his spirit lifted when he saw a dull glow appear in the window of the upper bedroom. Someone had lit a candle.

Basil kept running until he reached the front porch of the house. The door swung open almost immediately. The barrel of a gun poked out of the darkness of the doorway. Then Basil heard a very welcome and familiar voice.

"Basil? Is that you? What is wrong? Why have you come here alone in the middle of the cold night?" His brother, James, lowered the gun and ran toward Basil.

Basil attempted to respond, but he was so winded that he could not take in enough air to make an intelligent sound. As he tried to speak, the sudden urge to vomit struck his throat. He fell to his knees, gagged, and expelled a puddle of clear bile onto the dry dust of the ground.

Ann Billingsley appeared at the door, cradling a baby in her left arm. "What is the matter, James?"

"It is Basil! Something is wrong with him. He has been running and cannot catch his breath. The boy is sick. Bring some water!"

Ann darted back inside the house. James knelt beside his brother and cupped the back of the boy's neck with his hand.

"Calm down, Basil. Everything will be all right. Just relax, now. Breathe."

Basil shook his head. "Everything ... is not ... all ... right." He continued to gasp for air.

"Slow down, Little Brother, and tell me what has happened. Did you run here all the way from home?"

Basil nodded. He took two deep, cleansing breaths. "You must ... bring help. Men have come ... guns and torches. Many men. Soldiers."

"Soldiers are at Papa's house?" James confirmed. "Why?"

Basil's breathing steadied just a bit. "I do not know. They knocked down the door. I saw Papa fall on the floor and hit his head." Tears streamed down the lad's cheeks. "I slipped out the window and ran here to get you. We have to help them!"

James' eyes widened in disbelief. "You went out on the

roof?" He patted his little brother in admiration and encouragement. "I am so proud of you, Basil! Did Papa send you?"

"No. The men have taken him ... and Mama." His breath was slowly returning. "They were searching the house, but still had not made it upstairs before I escaped. Walter sent me to get you. He said bring men and guns. He said that something bad was going to happen."

"Is Walter all right?"

Basil nodded and continued to cry. "He was fine when I left him ... but I don't know how he is now. They were destroying our house. I heard wood crashing and glass breaking. And as I ran into the trees, I heard Martha screaming." The lad's tears flowed and his shoulders shook as he sobbed. "Oh, James! What have I done? I should not have left them there. I should have helped them all escape. It is not right that I am the only one who got away."

James embraced the boy and held him tight. "It's all right, Basil. You did the right thing. You obeyed Walter. Do not worry. I will go immediately. I will awaken other men of the militia on my way into town."

Ann arrived immediately with a pewter mug full of cold water. Basil drank three-fourths of it and then poured the remainder on top of his head.

James placed his right hand on his brother's shoulder. "Basil, I need you to do one more thing. Do you have the strength to make it to Samuel's house and rouse him?"

Basil nodded. "I do now." He smiled and looked at James' beautiful wife. "Thank you, Ann."

"You are quite welcome, Basil. You had me worried."

James helped the boy to his feet. "There is no time to waste, Basil. Go and alert Samuel. You can ride back into town with him. I will see you there. Tell him to send one of the hired men to fetch John and Henry. Make sure our brothers know to bring their guns, and all of the men they can muster."

"Yes, James."

"Tell them we may have a fight on our hands this night."

"Yes, James."

Basil hugged his brother and then trotted down the wagon road toward Samuel's house. He disappeared quickly around a turn in the path. A few minutes later he saw the outline of the house's roof. Candles were already burning in the downstairs. Samuel was standing on the front porch, rifle in hand. Apparently, the chorus of barking dogs at James' house had awakened him. Basil repeated his account of the night's events, along with James' instructions to fetch John and Henry and the hired men.

Samuel commanded excitedly, "Basil, bring out two horses from the barn! I must get my coat and bags."

"Yes, Samuel."

Samuel added grimly, "I will also bring a pistol for you, Basil. You may have to join in this fight."

A cold shudder of fear shook Basil. He had never fired a pistol. He had never shot anything but rabbits, birds, and squirrels. The thought of shooting a human being frightened him tremendously. He could scarcely imagine it. But the image of his father being knocked to the floor filled his mind. He closed his eyes and imagined soldiers tearing apart his home. He heard in his thoughts the screams of his mother and sister. He felt confused, frightened, and angry ... but mostly, he felt angry. He wanted those horrible men gone from his house.

Samuel asked, "Are you all right, Little Brother?"

Basil nodded. "Yes, Samuel. If I have to, I will fight for Mama and Papa."

On the Road to Guilford Courthouse

BASIL BILLINGSLEY WAS RIDING full speed and clinging for dear life to the mane of his horse. He was riding bareback. Samuel and the hired men had not wasted time putting saddles on the horses. They had precious little time to spare.

The Billingsley brothers were just about to reach the edge of town. Samuel rode beside Basil. Three farm laborers rode behind them. The five riders were moving at top speed. Another cluster of riders was about fifty yards ahead of them. It was Basil's other two brothers, James and Henry, and five of their friends from the local Guilford County militia regiment.

All of the riders carried muskets and rifles at the ready. Basil grasped the scratchy hair of the horse's mane in his left hand. He slowly reached down with his right hand and felt the smooth brass and wood handle of the flintlock pistol that was tucked snugly inside his belt. He could scarcely believe that Samuel had given him a gun. He felt so grown up. He felt like a man. And yet, he also felt so very afraid.

Basil glanced ahead. He could see a few dim lights and a thin haze of smoke that hovered over the village of Guilford Courthouse. The flickering lights looked like torches. He remembered the flaming sticks that the men carried into his house. He shuddered with fear as he recalled the torch-wielding man who had searched for him in his back yard.

Basil was almost home. James and the other men riding ahead of him began to yell at their horses and urge them forward. All of the riders seemed to be picking up speed. He heard his brother James exclaim, "They have attacked our home, boys! Kill them all!"

Basil's mind reeled. He thought, "*Can this really be happening? Will there actually be a battle on my lawn?*"

The high-pitched, wailing screams of a woman reached Basil's ears. But it was not just any woman. He recognized his own mother's voice, shrieking in horror and pain.

Samuel glanced at Basil. His eyes were filled with rage. "Get ready, Little Brother! Hold on tight! Don't draw your pistol until we reach the yard. And don't shoot at anyone unless you see me shoot! Understand?"

Basil did not open his mouth. He merely nodded. He was too afraid to speak.

Samuel continued, "And whatever you do, don't shoot Mama and Papa! Keep an eye out for Walter and Martha, as well."

Basil nodded again. His fear was so great that his entire body trembled.

Suddenly, gunfire erupted up ahead of them. James and Henry and the other militiamen were fighting! Basil heard men yelling and screaming. The battle had begun!

Samuel kicked violently at the sides of his horse and yelled, "Hyah!" As he held the horse's mane with his left hand, he pulled a flintlock pistol from his belt with his right hand. He leaned forward to lay low over the neck of his horse. As the animal galloped on, he drew the hammer on his pistol back to full cock and prepared to fire. Basil imitated his brother. He did not draw his weapon, but he did lean forward and cling tightly to the neck of his horse.

Just ahead the area in front of Basil's house flashed with the bright yellow explosions of musket and pistol fire. The sharp crack of the exploding weapons echoed in the darkness. Men yelled. Some screamed in pain and fear.

Samuel led Basil and the other men in his group around the stone fence that marked the boundary of the Billingsley property. The front lawn of the Billingsley house was a scene of carnage and confusion. Basil saw several of the invading soldiers running throughout the yard, all of them searching for cover and attempting to hide from the deadly gunfire of the men on horseback. He heard his mother screaming and the explosions of at least a dozen gunshots. He jumped with surprise when Samuel fired his pistol. Indeed, Basil almost fell off of his horse. He looked quickly at Samuel and saw that his brother was tucking the still-smoking pistol into his belt. Simultaneously, he pulled his musket from a leather sheath that was tied around the horse's neck. Basil's eyes met Samuel's.

Samuel screamed, "What are you waiting for, Basil? Shoot! Anyone who is shooting back is your enemy!"

Basil nodded. He spun his horse around and faced the front door of his home. He heard more gunshots. A lead ball screeched as it passed dangerously close to his ear. He actually felt the wind of the projectile as it whizzed by him. He pulled the huge flintlock pistol from his belt with his right hand and then reached with his left hand to pull back the hammer. It was not easy. The mechanism was very tight and stiff. Finally, after much tugging, he felt the hammer click into place.

He scanned the yard for a target. He spotted a man to his left, near the edge of the trees. The fellow was pouring powder from a cartridge down the barrel of his musket. The man's face glowed in the light of the torches. His eyes were filled with fear. Basil lifted the heavy pistol with both hands and pointed it at the man. He squeezed the trigger.

Basil had not expected the weapon to recoil so violently. The pistol kicked with a mighty force, jerking his hands upward and backward over his head. He lost his balance and tumbled sideways off of the horse. He flipped upside-down in the air and then landed on his chest with a huge thud. His head bounced off of the ground. The pain was unimaginable, especially in his upper belly and lower chest. He could not move, and he could not breathe.

As the battle raged all around him, Basil wondered, *"Have I been shot?"*

4

THE FIGHT IS WON

Thankfully, Basil had not been shot. Instead, the impact of the fall knocked the wind out of him. His inability to get air into his lungs caused him to panic. Basil had never even thought about the process of breathing. It was simply something that his body accomplished on its own. But now that he could not coax his lungs to function, it seemed that breathing was *all* that he could think about. And the harder he tried to suck air into his lungs, the more panicked he became.

Basil rolled awkwardly onto his back, hoping that the change of position might help him breathe. He was becoming frantic. He looked all around for someone to help him, but it seemed that everyone was too busy shooting, running, or hiding. The yard was full of confusion, fire, blood, and death. Basil wanted to cry, but first he had to find his breath.

He thought, "*Calm down, Basil! You've had the wind knocked out of you before. Just relax. Stop thinking about it. The air will come.*"

Basil closed his eyes and attempted to calm his spirit. He

intentionally avoided all efforts to breathe. Instead, he counted slowly to ten, put his lips together, and attempted to blow every bit of air out of his lungs. When he reached the number ten, he slowly, deliberately, and calmly began to breathe in.

It worked! Refreshing, cool air poured through his mouth and nose and quickly filled his wind-starved lungs! Basil lay flat on his back in the grass, closed his eyes, and relished the life-giving air. Somehow, he managed to tune out all of the gunfire and screaming that surrounded him.

He thought, *"I'm done fighting. I will simply lie here and play dead until it is all over."*

The shrill scream of a woman echoed to Basil's left, drawing him back from his solitude. It was his mother! He scanned in the direction of the scream. He gasped when he saw his mother at the edge of the tree line. One of the invading militiamen held the helpless woman by the hair of her head. He was using her as a shield against gunfire as he made his retreat into the woods.

There was a flash of movement as a horse approached from Basil's right. He recognized the rider. It was his brother, Henry, charging full-speed toward their mother and her captor. Henry held a cocked pistol in his hand. Basil watched helplessly as the man holding his mother brought his own pistol to bear on Henry. The man's gun barked and immediately the galloping horse and Henry Billingsley tumbled haphazardly to the ground, throwing up a cloud of sod and dust.

Basil heard another scream. It, too, was a familiar voice. Across the lawn, he spotted his older brother, Walter, running toward his mother and her captor. Walter had a pistol in his hand. He was aiming the gun, and preparing to fire. Walter had only taken three steps when something stopped him mid-run. The boy spun slightly to his left and then collapsed onto the dusty ground. He did not move.

Basil screamed, "Walter! No!"

He tried to roll over onto his knees. He had to help his brother! But, his pain-ravaged body was still slow in responding. The violent fall from the horse had left him bruised and sore.

Suddenly, unexpectedly, there were no more gunshots. Basil glanced around the yard. A haze of gunpowder smoke hovered in the air. The enemy soldiers were all gone. Samuel was kneeling beside their mother. James was tending to Walter. John and the workers from the farm were trying to extract Henry from beneath his dead horse. The poor animal lay across the lower part of his body, crushing his legs and pinning them to the ground. Henry screamed in pain.

Basil slowly climbed to his feet. He scanned his front yard. The lifeless bodies of seven enemy soldiers lay sprawled upon the lawn. Then he noticed something peculiar about the big oak tree that stood outside his bedchamber window. There was something hanging in it. There was a person hanging in it! Basil's heart sank when he saw who it was. It was his papa, James Billingsley Sr., hanging by the neck from a rope.

His kind, loving papa was dead ... murdered by the men who had invaded his home during the night.

Basil was a brave boy. He had run over a mile in the frightening darkness of the night to fetch his brothers. He had ridden bareback on a galloping horse to return home and help his parents, brother, and sister. He had even carried a gun into battle and fired a shot at one of the men who had attacked his home.

Yes, Basil Billingsley was a very brave boy. But ... he was

still just a boy. He was a heartbroken, confused, and frightened nine-year-old. His father was dead. His brothers were injured. His mother was screaming and crying. He did not know what to do. So, he sat down on the cold ground, crossed his legs, buried his face in his hands, and cried.

ONCE HE HAD ENJOYED a good cry, Basil wanted something purposeful to do. He needed to stay busy and keep his mind off of the horrible things that he had just seen and experienced. He first attempted to help Walter, who had been wounded. The boy suffered a large gash on his scalp where an attacker's bullet had grazed his skull. He had been unconscious for several minutes. Basil hovered near the body of his wounded brother, attempting to awaken him. But it seemed that all he was really doing was getting in the way of the grown-ups. James politely shooed his little brother away, urging him to go and find something else to do. Basil was heartbroken, but he obeyed his big brother.

At long last, he received a worthy task to perform. Samuel placed Basil in charge of their mother's care. Elizabeth Billingsley was in very bad shape. She was physically and emotionally injured. Basil simply hugged her for a while. Actually, they embraced one another. Basil could not be sure who enjoyed the hugs more ... him or his mother. But, eventually, he encouraged her to follow him inside the house. Basil seated her in a rocking chair beside the fireplace and stoked the coals from the previous evening's fire.

Soon, his sister Martha came and helped attend to her mother's needs, as well. Amazingly, with Walter's help, Martha had managed to escape from the invading soldiers and hide in the woods. Once the battle was over, she returned to the safety of her home. She suffered several scratches and bruises while running through the dark forest, but was otherwise uninjured.

Minutes later, the local doctor arrived at the Billingsley home. Martha helped the physician clean and bandage her mother's cuts and scrapes. She helped her mother put on a clean nightgown, and then brushed her hair. Basil busied himself by preparing his mother's bed and brewing her some hot tea. All the while, the dazed woman never spoke or responded to their actions. She simply sat and stared numbly at the flames of the fireplace.

Basil could not imagine the pain that filled his mother's heart. He knew that his own heart was shattered by his father's violent death. The boy had watched tearfully when his brothers cut the rope and carefully lowered their father's body from the tree. He could not imagine the loss that his mother felt. His parents had been together for over thirty years. They had spent their entire lifetimes together. How would she ever be able to continue on and live her life without him?

As he stirred a spoonful of sugar into his mother's teacup, Basil shook his head in anger and disgust. Large, heavy teardrops flowed down his cheeks. He could not imagine why anyone would wish to hurt his beloved, kindly father. Basil felt bitter and vengeful and confused. He wanted to understand why all of this had happened to his family.

Basil carried the fresh tea into his mother's bedchamber. He arrived in the room just as Martha was tucking her mother into her soft feather bed. Suddenly, a shrill cry carried across the front lawn. It was the voice of Gabriel Tate, one of the farm workers, and Walter Billingsley's best friend.

Gabriel excitedly exclaimed, "Walter is awake! He is all right! Come and see!"

Basil glanced pleadingly at his sister. He desperately wanted to go and check on the well-being of his brother. And he wanted answers. He wanted to know why his home had been attacked, and why these horrible things had happened to his family.

Martha smiled. "Go ahead, Little Brother. I will help Mama with her tea and then sit with her until she goes to sleep. I will come and see Walter as soon as I can."

Basil grinned thankfully. He quickly sat the cup on his mother's nightstand, kissed his sister on the cheek, and then sprinted out of the house. He ran to the spot where Walter still lay on the ground. The boy was surrounded by all of his older brothers. Basil broke through the circle and fell upon Walter, covering him with a barrage of squeals and hugs.

"Slow down there, Basil," urged Samuel. "Walter's been slugged. A bullet bounced off of his skull." The eldest Billingsley brother peeled Basil off of his wounded sibling. The four siblings knelt in a brotherly circle of protection and care. Gabriel Tate hovered over Samuel's left shoulder.

"What happened to those men who killed Papa?" Walter asked bluntly.

"Tory hooligans," Samuel corrected him. "Bushwhackers and robbers loyal to King George!" He spat on the ground.

"I know who and what they are, Sam. Now tell me ... what happened to them?"

"Seven of them won't see another sunrise," commented John. "Another five or six stole away into the woods. We found the horses of the dead tied off in a small cove about two hundred yards to the west."

Walter nodded slightly. "There were thirteen total, as best I could tell. Their captain and another dozen men."

Samuel nodded. "That's what we calculated."

"Did you get their captain?" hissed Walter.

James responded, "I don't think so. The dead men all look like ordinary fellows. From the looks of their clothes, they were all farmers ... and poor ones, at that. Which one was their captain?"

"The one that had Mama by the hair of her head," responded Walter, his lip quivering.

"Oh ... so he was the one that shot Henry's horse," mumbled Samuel.

Walter nodded slightly. "Will Henry be all right? I saw him fall."

Samuel smiled. "He'll be fine. Doc says he might carry a limp for the rest of his days, but he will still be able to swing an axe and a hoe."

James commented, "Walter, I saw you going after Mama. You were running, pistol in hand, and then I saw you lurch and go down hard. I assumed that the fellow who had Mama was the one who shot you."

Walter shook his head slowly. "No, he had just gotten off a shot at Henry, so his powder was spent. I was too afraid to shoot. He was holding Mama right up against him. I was making a move to his left, and trying to get closer, when I felt a loud thump on my head. The next thing I knew, Gabe was dangling over me and chattering a mile a minute."

The Billingsley brothers chuckled lightly. Gabriel Tate feigned a look of offense.

"Where did you get the pistol?" inquired Samuel.

Walter remained silent for a moment, and then answered, "Off of the man that I killed ... the one over by the steps."

The men in the circle glanced knowingly at one another.

"I saw you taking cover behind the body when I arrived,"

commented James. "I was wondering what had happened. You killed him with your bare hands, didn't you?"

Walter nodded. He responded just above a mumble, his words choked by emotion. "I'm so very sorry that I couldn't save Papa." His lip quivered as more tears welled in his eyes.

"There were too many of them, Walter. What more could you have done?" encouraged James.

"I don't know." His body shook slightly. He paused and glanced toward the hanging tree. His voice became somewhat frantic. "Where is Papa? Who took him?"

"We cut him down, Walter," James assured him, placing his hand on his brother's shoulder. "Papa is being cared for. Some of the ladies from the church are cleaning him up proper so that we can have a service for him tomorrow."

Walter nodded, his face displaying relief.

Basil could remain silent no longer. He pleaded, "But, why did they do this, Walter? Why did these men come after us? Why did they hang Papa?"

Walter stared empty-eyed at his little brother. He reached up and rubbed the hair on Basil's head. "It is complicated, Basil. I am not certain that you would understand."

"I am not stupid, Walter. I know more than you think I do. Now, tell me!" Basil demanded.

Walter glanced at his older brothers. "They said he was guilty of treason against the King."

"That doesn't make any sense!" exclaimed Samuel. "Papa is not involved in politics or the legislature! How could he commit treason against England?"

Walter explained, "Their captain acted like a crazy man. He accused Papa of hiding weapons and terrorists in our home. Papa swore up and down that he was not a traitor. He told the man that he was, most definitely, not hiding weapons in our house. A few minutes later one of the soldiers upstairs got all excited when he found my hunting gun."

"Grandpa's old bird gun?" asked John in disbelief.

Walter nodded. "Once they found the gun, the captain declared that Papa had lied to him. He said that Papa had lied to the King. He called him a traitor to the Crown. He demanded that Papa surrender a fine of one hundred pounds sterling in silver to pay for his so-called crimes."

Gabriel Tate whistled low under his breath. The Billingsley boys exhaled in disbelief.

"And all this was over an ancient bird gun?" growled James.

Walter shook his head in disgust, ignoring the throbbing pain in his skull.

"No, it was more than that. I think the man intended to hang Papa all along. He was just looking for an excuse," replied Walter.

"Did he hurt you, Walter?" Basil asked innocently.

Walter smiled reassuringly. "I said a couple of unkind words to him. He clubbed me over the head with his pistol. But, don't worry, I will be just fine."

"It's a good thing that your head is made of iron," teased Basil.

Walter punched his little brother lightly in the arm. "Well, they surely were not expecting you fellows to show up," declared Walter. "They paid for that mistake, didn't they?"

"Indeed, they did," affirmed James. He paused and then patted Walter gently on the chest. "That was good thinking, by the way ... sending Basil out the window to alert the rest of us." He glanced at Basil. "And I can't believe that you ran all that way in the middle of the night, Little Brother."

Basil beamed with pride.

James continued, "I know that our Papa is dead, and my heart is broken because of it. But the two of you likely saved both Mama and Martha."

"And Lord knows who else these men might have intended to attack," added John. "It was a brave thing that you lads accomplished this night."

Samuel nodded. "Brave, indeed. Who would have ever thought that Walter and Basil would have been the first among us to fight in this war of revolution?"

An awkward silence hovered over the group.

Gabriel Tate slapped Samuel on the back and inserted himself into the moment. "Well, you Billingsley boys can all hold hands and kiss later. How's about we get Walter inside out of the cold night and tend to him proper? Besides, it will be time for breakfast soon, and I'm famished! One of you fellows is going have to do a wee bit of cooking! I like gravy with my biscuits!"

The Billingsley brothers, despite the pain in their hearts, laughed at the ever-entertaining Gabe Tate. They helped Walter to his feet, hugged one another, and then walked around the back of the house toward the kitchen. As they journeyed toward a warm fire and the promise of hot food, young Basil prayed that a good meal and the fellowship of his brothers might help him forget about the horrible events of this dreadful night.

PART II

MAN OF THE HOUSE - 1780

5

THE BEAST

May 1, 1780

"**I**t will be dark in an hour," Basil thought. He sighed. "*I shall have to head for home soon.*"

The impatient fifteen-year-old muttered out loud, "Another wasted afternoon!"

He heard a twig snap somewhere to his left. His heart skipped a beat.

"*Billingsley!*" he scolded himself mentally. "*You just spooked a deer!*"

At least, he hoped that it was a deer. A fat, tasty doe would be a great blessing, indeed, for his family. And how proud he would be to bring such a prize home to his mother!

Basil, lounging lazily against the trunk of a small oak tree, sat upright and raised his Pennsylvania fowling gun to the ready. The old flintlock was loaded with a round ball and four smaller pieces of buckshot ... plenty of lead to bring down a deer critter. He listened carefully and tried to control his breathing. His heart thumped loudly in his chest. He continued to scan the trail to his left that led to the nearby salt lick. It was a popular place for the local does to visit in the late afternoon. After several silent, still minutes he shook his head, disappointed, and gave up. Again, he slumped back against the soft, cool moss that coated the base of the tree.

The Billingsleys needed fresh meat. They were not starving or desperate, by any means, but their winter stores were beginning to run low. The potatoes and pumpkins were all consumed by mid-February. Precious few of the dried vegetables and jarred fruits remained. The various Patriot militias that roamed the forests and fields of Guilford and Randolph Counties had purchased or confiscated a large portion of their cows and hogs. At least their chicken and egg supplies were sufficient, if not ample.

But Basil was growing weary of eating chicken and eggs. Lately, the most common addition to their diet was mushrooms foraged from the forest floor ... and Basil hated mushrooms. He positively gagged at the salads that his mother made from the leaves and flowers of the dandelions that grew in nearby pastures. Their Quaker neighbors had recently introduced his mother to this strange, new food source.

His older brothers helped their mother as much as they could, but they were having difficulty providing for the needs of their own families. Besides, Basil really did not want their help. He was the man of the house now, and he took very seriously his responsibility to provide for his mother and sister, Martha. It was a matter of personal pride for the scrappy youth.

If they could just hold out a bit longer, there would be

plenty of food in a few months. That was certain. Due to the hard work of Basil's mother and sister, the family gardens were progressing nicely. Still, it would be a few weeks before the tomatoes, squashes, and cucumbers would begin to bear. Beans would not be ready until July. Their apple, pear, plum, and peach orchards would not begin to produce fruit until early August. And it would be September before Basil's older brothers would reap a harvest of potatoes, wheat, and corn from the rich fields of the Billingsley farmland.

But the promise of plenty at summer's end did precious little to quell the hunger that the Billingsleys would suffer in the days and weeks to come. Basil needed to bring home some fresh game for the table. The occasional rabbit, turkey, or squirrel was helpful. But he really wanted to impress his mother and sister. He wanted big game. He dreamed of shooting a deer or, even better, an elk. Surely, a generous supply of meat for the drying rack and smokehouse would do much to raise spirits at home. It would also show Basil's mother that he truly was a man, and quite capable of providing for the needs of their household.

The four years that had passed since that fateful, deadly Tory raid on their home had been difficult ones for the Billingsleys. The rebellion against England had cost their family dearly.

James Billingsley had been slain during that horrible raid. Henry Billingsley was permanently crippled, his leg crushed by his fallen horse. Walter was gravely injured and required almost a year to recover from his wounds. Yet, the events of that horrible night were only the beginning. The American Revolution continuously impacted Elizabeth Billingsley and her sons and daughters throughout the next four years.

The widowed Elizabeth had watched helplessly as her three oldest sons marched off to war. Samuel, James, and John all served in the great Cherokee Campaign of the autumn of 1776. Walter, though he had desperately wanted to go and serve with his brothers, heeded his mother's demands and remained at home in her care. Basil was glad that he had stayed home. Despite their regular arguments and spats, Walter was his closest brother and very best friend. He loved him dearly.

After returning home from the Cherokee Campaign, each of the older brothers served several three-month enlistments in their local militia regiments. Though there had been no actual British to fight, there was a constant threat from British Loyalists ... the Tories. Small groups from South Carolina and eastern North Carolina occasionally made raids into the Piedmont. It seemed that one of the Billingsley boys was always away on militia duty, either on cavalry patrol, guarding Tory prisoners, or escorting supply convoys through the region.

Walter relentlessly continued to pester his mother about militia service, but all of that changed on an autumn afternoon in 1778. That was when Abigail Hamer entered Walter's life. The young maiden from South Carolina, visiting in the home of a Billingsley relative, had completely upended Walter's world.

The young couple fell helplessly, hopelessly in love. After only one week of courtship, the love-struck pair was already making marriage plans. They simply had to wait a few years for Walter to reach legal marrying age. Meanwhile, they nurtured their all-consuming romance by writing endless letters. Walter also managed to find ways to visit Abigail from time to time at her hometown of Camden, South Carolina.

But Walter, now eighteen years of age, was the most recent of the Billingsley boys to travel into harm's way. He departed ten days prior for Camden, South Carolina ... but not to go to war. He went there to fetch home his beautiful fiancé, Abigail, to the relative safety of North Carolina. The British had recently landed their army at Charlestown, and were threatening to break out of the ring of Continental Army soldiers that surrounded the city. Once their Dragoons were on the loose, Camden would surely be one of their targets.

Walter was not taking any chances. He simply had to go and get his beloved Abigail and bring her home. He had to protect his future bride. Walter did not feel that he could wait any longer. His plan was simple ... he would bring Abigail back to Guilford County, they would be wed immediately, and then they would live in a newly-constructed cottage on the Billingsley farm. Walter had been working on the house for over a year, with help from Basil and the other brothers. It was a charming little cottage, and almost complete.

Basil smiled as he remembered watching Walter and his clownish friend, Gabriel Tate, riding off in the family wagon on the road toward Salisbury. They were certain to have a great adventure! He was happy for his brother, and a bit envious. He was also a bit sad about the notion of his brother leaving home and moving to his own house on the family farm.

Basil suddenly felt a wave of loneliness wash across his soul. He could not even remember any of his other brothers living at home with him. They were all wed when Basil was very young. Indeed, Samuel had been married before Basil was even born! But Walter had always been there for him. The two of them had grown up together. Even though they

fussed and fought constantly, they had always been inseparable. Basil's heart ached at the thought of sleeping alone in
a room with three empty beds in it. Surely, the coming years
would be filled with many lonely days and nights.

A strange, pungent odor invaded Basil's nostrils and
snatched him away from his wandering thoughts. The
leaves near his head rustled, evidence of the breeze that had
carried the unpleasant smell. The odor was strong and
musky. It was not the smell of death or rot. It reminded Basil
of his old Billy goat that he had played with as a young
child.

"What, in Heaven's name, is that smell?" he wondered.

Suddenly, the forest grew very quiet. The birds that filled
the canopy of trees has ceased their cheerful, chirping
songs. Squirrels no longer frolicked, jumped, or chattered.
There were no sounds of life, at all. The only thing that
remained was the dull rustle of limbs and leaves swaying in
the breeze high overhead. The hair on Basil's neck stood on
end. A shiver of fear and uncertainty tickled across his back.
Then, it seemed, even the wind stopped blowing. There was
absolute, dead silence.

"What is going on?" whispered Basil, confused. *"This is
most strange!"*

The silence of the forest was shattered by a loud grunt
immediately behind Basil's hiding place. Then the bushes
behind him began to shake. The rank odor became overwhelming. He spun to his left to discover the source of the
noise and the smell. The sight that greeted him almost
made his heart stop.

He was staring directly into the face of a bear! The
beast's snout was barely a foot away from Basil's own nose.
The animal did not seem to be disturbed at the sight of a

human. Indeed, if anything, it was curious. It inhaled deeply, sniffing the boy's head. It snorted playfully, hurling a mist of moist air and snot into Basil's face.

Basil reacted to the animal out of shock and fear. Though the bear showed no signs of aggression or attack, the frightened boy instinctively jerked away and swung the stock of his Fowler gun upward. The weapon struck the bear soundly in the chin. It was a well-aimed, vicious blow. The hard brass of the butt-plate impacted a tooth that protruded from the bear's upper lip. There was a loud cracking sound. The shattered tooth flew from the animal's mouth and bounced off of the tree. Basil fell backwards.

The bear was stunned for a moment. It shook its head in confusion. Droplets of blood leaked from its wounded mouth. Immediately, the bear abandoned its curious, harmless sniffing. It rose high on its haunches and growled in pain and anger. It lunged ferociously at Basil. Its claws dug deeply into the small tree against which he had been resting. Chunks of dislodged bark and dust rained down on the frightened boy. The bear shook the tree violently, dislodging leaves, dust, pollen, and insects from its canopy. The falling debris added to Basil's terror and confusion.

Basil was petrified with fear. Black bears were still relatively common in the forests and mountains of western North Carolina. However, hunters and settlers did not encounter them very often in Guilford County. John Billingsley shot a bear several years ago on the family farm. Basil remembered that event very well, because it was such a rarity in the Piedmont region. Basil had never even seen a bear in the wild, much less had a personal encounter with one.

Suddenly, Basil remembered the gun in his hands. He

pushed himself backward, away from the bear, and attempted to aim the weapon at the wailing, growling animal. The bear sensed his aggression, dropped down onto all four of its legs, and slapped angrily at the gun barrel. Its claws scarred the wood and jarred the gun loose from Basil's hands. It slammed against the tree and fell to the ground. The beast gave a mighty, angry roar, spraying Basil with a mixture of foul saliva and blood.

Once again, the bear rose up onto its hind legs and shook the nearby tree and bushes. It was in pain, and making every attempt to frighten away the curious-looking, pale human that had caused its discomfort. It did not appear that it wanted to fight. It was merely making a show of force ... and making a lot of noise. The bear lifted its head upward and roared at the treetops as it continued to shake the foliage.

Basil took advantage of the bear's change of posture and lapse in attention. Though he was lying flat on his back, he reached to his left and grabbed his gun from the ground. He pulled the hammer back to full cock and thrust the barrel toward the bear. At that exact moment, the raging beast once again dropped down on all four legs and took a step through the bushes toward Basil. It opened its mouth and emitted another thunderous roar. The horrified boy thrust the barrel of the flintlock deep into the bear's open mouth and instantly pulled the trigger.

The sound of the explosion was deafening. The gunpowder pan of the weapon was just below Basil's chin. The explosive powder blew a cloud of fire and smoke upward into his face. He could feel the scorch of sparks against his chin and cheeks. He turned his head, gagged and coughed, attempting to coax a breath of fresh air from outside the cloud of bitter smoke. His ears were ringing loudly. Something very heavy was pinning his legs to the ground. Basil realized that flames were coming from the sleeve of his hunting frock on his right arm. He released the gun and slapped at the fire with his left hand, extinguishing the flames quickly.

It took a couple of seconds for the smoke to clear. A slight breeze scattered the smoke just enough for him to catch a glimpse of the bear. Basil stared toward his legs and feet in disbelief. The beast lay still. It was belly-down, with its chest on top of Basil's legs. The animal's bloody snout was just below his crotch. The gun barrel hung loosely from its silent mouth.

The bear was dead. Basil was alive. The boy's body shook from fear. He threw his burned, smoky forearm over his face, sucked in a heaving breath, and cried.

SAMUEL AND JOHN BILLINGSLEY stared at the carcass of the bear. Basil stood proudly beside the animal, his gun cradled lazily in the crook of his left arm. Both men cast a somewhat incredulous glance at their little brother.

"And the critter fell on you when you shot it?" questioned Samuel in disbelief, pointing at Basil's bloody breeches.

Basil nodded. He did not feel much like talking. He was tired, having run all the way to Samuel's house to tell him about his kill.

"You let it get that close to you before you shot it?" John asked.

Basil's head hung a bit low. "I never even heard the bear until it stuck its head into the thicket where I was hiding."

"Were you asleep, Little Brother?" challenged John.

"No!" Basil answered emphatically. "I was not asleep!"

"What were you doing, then, that would so occupy your mind, that you could not hear a four-hundred-pound bear walk up to you?"

Basil shrugged his shoulders. "I was thinking, I suppose."

"Thinking?" challenge Samuel, almost shouting. "About what?"

"Oh, I do not know. About Walter, mostly. About him getting married and moving out of the house, and me being left there ... alone ... with two women."

Samuel chuckled. "There are a lot worse places to be in this world than at home, snug and safe, with Mother. I can assure you of that."

John grunted and nodded in agreement.

Samuel continued, "But I can see how such change could be troubling to you. Change can do that to a man. But you cannot let change or your fear of it defeat you, Basil. Do you understand? You have to keep your mind focused on what is truly important and just keep on moving forward."

John grinned. "Then, one of these days soon, you shall be wedded and moving out on your own, just like Walter."

Basil blushed, embarrassed, and covered his hand with his mouth.

"Anyhow, you have other things to worry about right now, Little Brother," encouraged Samuel. "You have killed yourself a fine, big bear. Now we have some work to do. We have to get this huge beast back to Mother's barn, skin it, trim the fat for rendering, and butcher the meat. I will wager that there are over two hundred pounds of fine meat on that critter. Maybe another twenty or thirty beyond that."

John walked over and put his arms around Basil's shoulders. "But, do not worry, Basil. We shall help you clean it ... and eat it." He grinned warmly at the tired boy.

"Indeed!" chirped Samuel. "We must get word to our brothers and their families. We shall gather the entire Billingsley clan this night! It will be a feast of roast bear ... courtesy of our little brother, Basil!"

6

THE LETTER

May 6, 1780

"Walter is going to love this!" Basil exclaimed.

He stepped back, wiping the dust from his hands on his workman's apron, and surveyed his handiwork. A single bear claw dangled proudly from a leather thong around his neck. It was his only reminder of the frightening beast that he had killed in the woods near his home.

Basil had just finished adding decorative wood trim along the edges of the ceiling in Walter's cottage. The new wood molding was perfect. Indeed, it was stunning. The dark brown stain of the decorative oak contrasted perfectly with the clean, whitewashed walls. It looked very refined and fancy.

Basil grinned. Yes, Walter and Abigail would be very proud!

Luxuries such as this fine wood molding were a rarity among households on the edge of the Carolina frontier.

They were difficult to mill and produce, and very expensive to purchase. Most ordinary folk simply could not afford such luxuries. Basil had noticed Walter admiring some of the beautiful trim molding on one of their visits to the sawmill at New Market, the largest Quaker settlement in Guilford County. The price was extremely high, and far outside of Walter's budget. Still, Basil noticed how much his big brother had stared longingly at the exquisite wood.

So, after shooting the bear, Basil decided to devise a bit of a surprise for Walter. He loaded his prized bear hide into Henry's wagon, along with four quart jars of freshly rendered bear grease, and headed off to New Market in search of a trade. Bear furs and fat were something of a rare and precious commodity in Guilford County. The grease of a bear was the perfect lubricant for the cloth patches used in the barrels of hunting rifles. It was also used to soften and moisten leather for making saddles, straps, and bags. The bear skin would, of course, make an excellent bedcover or rug.

As it turned out, the trade with the Quaker miller came quite easily. The owner of the sawmill in New Market, Mordecai Starbuck, was anxious to procure a supply of bear grease. His brother and business partner, Philemon, was a well-known and respected leather worker. He produced saddles, riding gear, belts, and bags for most of the local stores. It was clear that Mordecai also coveted the large, luxurious bear skin. He had never seen such a fine fur before.

It took very little haggling for Basil to successfully obtain one hundred and ten feet of the wood trim. That was plenty to complete both the upstairs and downstairs of Walter's cottage, with just a little to spare. Mr. Starbuck even included a special jig for cutting the corners of the wood molding so that they would match perfectly.

While he was in New Market, Basil made one more trade. He bartered the remaining bear claws, along with the animal's teeth, to the local blacksmith in exchange for ten pounds of small finishing nails. He was certain that would be enough to complete the job.

It had taken him all day to finish his work. He measured and re-measured every single piece of the molding. He used the jig to cut the corner pieces with absolute precision. He definitely did not want to make any "bad cuts" and waste any of the precious wood. His tools had functioned flawlessly. His measurements were perfect. He could not have been more pleased.

"Enough carpentry for today!" he declared. "I am ready for some supper!"

He secured all of his woodworking tools in Walter's storage shed, quickly strapped his English saddle onto the back of his spunky mare, Geneva, and then guided the animal along the trail toward the homes of his older brothers. They lived less than a quarter-mile from Walter's cottage. Basil knew that Samuel was scheduled to serve a three-month enlistment in the militia soon, and he wanted to see him before he departed.

Basil soon caught sight of the rooftop of Samuel's house. He had many fond memories in that old home. It was actually the first house that his father had built when he brought the family to North Carolina from Baltimore, Maryland. Basil had spent most of his childhood in that house. He actually liked it better than their new, brick home in Guilford. Samuel and his wife, Mary, took ownership of the farmhouse when James and Elizabeth Billingsley moved into town in the spring of 1774.

He cupped his hands to his face and called out, "Hello, in the house!"

The door flew open and four small children ran out into the yard. There were three little girls and one boy. All of them squealed with delight.

Little Samuel, age five, chirped, "Uncle Basil! Have you come to play?"

Basil grinned. He climbed down from his horse and looped the reins across the limb of a small bush. He knelt on the ground and welcomed the four children as they swamped him with a wave of hugs.

"No, Sam, I do not have time to play. I have been working on Walter's house, and just stopped by to visit with your papa for a bit."

"Papa is gone," declared Sarah, age seven.

"He left just after dinner today," added her twin sister, Mary.

"Where did he go?"

Samuel's wife, Mary, appeared at the door of the house. "The militia got called up early, Basil. He and John departed in a hurry at mid-day."

Basil's smile disappeared. He stood upright and shooed the children away. "Why all the rush?"

"Their captain received word of a Tory attack over in northern Rowan County. Their regiment left in pursuit of the raiders." Mary frowned. "He barely had time to pack anything."

"Maybe they will not be gone very long," Basil encouraged.

Mary sighed. "I hope not. The work is quite overwhelming around here whenever Samuel is gone." She rubbed her large belly. She was expecting their fifth child.

"When will the baby come?" asked Basil, worried.

Mary smiled reassuringly. "Not for another month, at least. But doing the basic tasks here around the house is getting harder. Little Samuel and the twins are a big help, but there is only so much they can do."

"Well, I will help all that I can. I will come by every afternoon to check on you," Basil promised.

Mary nodded. "I will be most grateful, Basil. I am sure that Jean would appreciate a visit, as well. She is so unhappy and so overwhelmed when John is gone."

Basil grinned. "I will be sure to check on her, too." He glanced around the yard. "Do you need anything right now?"

"I hate to ask you, Basil ... but I could really use a load of split wood in the kitchen. And the milk cow is probably about to burst wide open."

"It will be my pleasure to assist you, Madam." Basil bowed teasingly. "I shall relieve the burdened cow first, and then attend to the firewood."

"A couple of buckets of fresh water would be a big help, as well," Mary pleaded.

"Consider it done, milady!" Basil tapped little Samuel on the head. "Sam, go and fetch your hat, and then join me in the barn. We shall have us a milking lesson."

"Yes, sir, Uncle Basil!" The boy bounced excitedly toward the door of the house.

Mary smiled warmly. "I sincerely thank you, Basil. You do not know how much this means to me."

Basil nodded with all seriousness and sincerity. "It is the least that I can do, Mary. You are family, after all."

He turned and marched toward the barn. He spent the next hour, with nephew Sam at his side, catching up on the many chores that his brother, Samuel, left undone due to his hasty departure for the war. As Basil worked, he prayed fervently for their success in battle ... and for their safety.

Once all of the chores were complete, Basil once again received a flood of hugs and kisses from Samuel's children as he prepared to mount his horse for the ride home. He leapt onto the animal's back, tipped his hat to his grateful sister-in-law, and then turned the mare in the direction of his house. It would only take a few minutes to make the quick one-mile trip back home. He just hoped that his mother had a hot supper hanging in the fireplace. He had worked up quite an appetite since breakfast. He whistled a happy tune as he leisurely guided his trusty horse toward the comforts of home.

BASIL BURST loudly through the back door of the Billingsley house. "Mother! What is going on? There is no smoke coming from the kitchen. What is for supper? I am famished!"

He rounded the corner from the hallway into the parlor and discovered his mother and sister, Martha, locked in a sobbing embrace. Basil was thoroughly confused.

"Mother! Martha! What is the matter?"

The beautiful maiden, Martha, pulled away from her despondent mother.

"Oh, Basil!" she sobbed. "It is positively awful!"

"What is awful?" he demanded. "What has happened?"

"It is Walter! Poor Walter!" Martha replied.

Basil's heart leapt in his chest. What manner of tragedy had befallen his brother and very best friend?

"What is the matter with Walter? Is he injured?" Basil

gulped. "He is not dead, is he?" Tears began to form in the corners of his eyes. His body shuddered and trembled.

Elizabeth Billingsley rose quickly to her feet and moved toward her son. "Oh, no, Basil! He is not injured or dead. But the army has taken him."

"The army? What army? Have the British impressed him into service?" Basil blurted angrily.

Elizabeth wiped a tear from her cheek with a silk handkerchief. "No, dear. Not the British. Virginians. Continental Army Regulars in Salisbury."

Basil's mind reeled. It did not make any sense! What would the Continental Army want with Walter? He was simply going to Camden to fetch home his fiancé and marry her.

"I do not understand, Mother. How can the Continental Army simply take a man? They do not do such things. I know that the British enlist people against their will, but I have never heard of impressment by our own Patriot armies."

Elizabeth turned and retrieved a piece of paper from the mahogany table beside the front window.

"Your brother sent me a letter," she declared. "It does not reveal much, but it should help you understand what has happened."

Basil, hands trembling, took the letter from his mother. He reverently unfolded it and began to read.

My Dearest Mother,

I am writing you to inform you of a great misfortune that has befallen me on my trek to Camden. I encountered soldiers from Virginia, encamped near Salisbury, who desired to confiscate our wagon and horses on the public roadway. I refused their orders and attempted to proceed on my way, but was apprehended and taken into custody. The army has, indeed, taken ownership of our wagon and team for military use.

In our attempt to flee, Gabriel and I apparently injured one of their men. He was not injured seriously, but it was enough to cause them to regard us as criminals. In lieu of pressing formal charges against us, the military authorities gave us the option of enlisting in the Virginia Line. They demanded that we choose between jail in Virginia or service in the army. Needless to say, we are both now soldiers encamped here with the Virginians. I have been compelled into enlistment for a period of three years, or until the end of the war. I believe that we will march to Charlestown very soon.

Thus far, I have been unable to get word to Abigail. There have been no postal riders dispatched to the south for several days. Please, if you are able, write to her and inform her of my predicament. Please make her understand that none of this is of my own choosing. I simply could not endure incarceration in the North.

Please tell her that I am very sorry, and that I will contact her as soon as I am able. Gabriel is here with me as I am writing to you. He would be most grateful if you could inform his family regarding our situation.

Pray for me, Dearest Mother, as I am greatly afraid of the fate that awaits me on the battlefield. Pray that I might see home again and that my marriage, though delayed, still awaits me in the not-too-distant future.

Your Devoted Son,
Walter

Basil slowly lowered the letter. His mind reeled. He was

sick with worry for his brother. He stared wide-eyed at his mother.

"The British have Charlestown under siege, Mother," Basil stated flatly.

"I know, Son."

"The city will fall soon ... everyone says so."

His mother nodded. "Indeed. I have heard the same predictions."

Basil blinked. "Once the British Regulars are out of Charlestown, there will be all-out war in the Carolinas. Walter will surely be involved."

"I know, Basil."

The boy took a deep breath. "I must go and join him. Gabriel Tate will be of no use to Walter, whatsoever. Gabe is a good friend to Walter, but he is a fool. I daresay he will run from the first sign of danger. I will stand and fight with Walter."

"You will do no such thing!" retorted his mother. "I shall not allow it! You are only fifteen years old. I will not give my consent, and the army will not take you without it."

"But, Mother!"

"You will heed my word, Basil Billingsley!" she scolded him. "Besides, what would Martha and I do without you? You are the sole provider for this household. Your brothers are helpful, but your sister and I rely upon you."

Martha rose and walked to Basil. "Mother is right, Little Brother. The war is no place for you. We do, indeed, need you here to take care of us." She wrapped her arms around his neck. "It breaks my heart to watch James and John and Samuel march off to war every few months. And now we have Walter to worry over, as well." She shook her head. "No, Basil. You must remain here at home. Mother needs you. I need you."

Basil sniffed and raised his shoulders proudly. "I shall abide by your wishes, Mother ... for now. But when I am of age, I plan to join the militia in Guilford County and fight alongside my brothers."

"I pray that, by the grace of God, this horrible war will be over and done before that day comes," Elizabeth declared.

7

THIEF IN THE NIGHT

August 16, 1780

Basil stepped out of the pre-dawn darkness into the warm glow of the kitchen. He slammed the door angrily. After dropping an empty tin feed bucket loudly onto the floor, he stomped in the direction of his favorite chair. He mumbled as he strode, "I am going to catch them! I swear ... I am going to catch them! And when I catch them, I am going to kill them with my bare hands!" He plopped into the chair and then glared angrily out the window.

His sister, Martha, took a break from kneading a pile of bread dough and cast a disbelieving glance at her mother. Elizabeth was checking to see if the breakfast porridge was fully cooked. She tapped her tasting spoon on the side of the pot, slowly pushed it closer to the flames of the fireplace, and then turned and faced her son. She placed both fists firmly on her hips. The twinkling firelight glistened in her eye, revealing her displeasure with her son's vulgar outburst.

"Basil Billingsley, I will not tolerate such talk of violence in my own house. Do you understand me?"

"Yes, mother." He stomped his foot. "But another one of my hens is gone!"

Elizabeth's stern look softened just a bit. She lowered her hands from her hips and took a step toward her son.

"How many have you lost?"

"Seven ... in just as many days."

"And you are certain that they are not simply escaping?"

Basil rolled his eyes dramatically. "No, Mother. Chickens are not known to escape in the dark of night. Once they go to roost, they remain until morning."

Elizabeth's eyes opened wide, surprised once again at the boy's disrespectful eye roll. "And you are certain that it is not a predator of some sort? A fox, perhaps?"

"Most definitely not. There is no blood or any other sign of violence ... not even loose feathers. Someone is robbing us, Mother. The enclosure is closed and locked each evening and morning, and yet, one chicken disappears every single night. It is the handiwork of a man ... a thief."

"Whatever shall you do? Surely, this cannot continue. How many hens do we have left?" queried Martha, pounding the pile of bread dough with her fist.

"I am not yet certain what I should do." Basil frowned. "I counted nineteen birds this morning. We only had eleven eggs yesterday. At this rate, we will be cleared out by the end of next week."

"Are any of the hens broody and sitting on eggs?" his mother asked, as she resumed her breakfast preparations.

"Just one," Basil mumbled. "She has been sitting for just over a week now. I moved her to the smokehouse and stuffed two dozen eggs beneath her, so we should have chicks in less than two weeks." He looked concerned. "But that will be of little use to us if we lose all of our layers.

We need our eggs. No one is selling or trading any right now."

Elizabeth sighed. "Well, if there is a thief on the loose, he must be apprehended. It could be a vagrant, or a wayward Indian. Shall I inform the sheriff?"

Basil laughed sarcastically. "Sheriff Bingham? The 'hero' who hid behind a tree whilst the Tories hanged Papa four years ago?" He snorted with disgust. "Not likely! No, this is my responsibility. I will take care of it on my own. I will catch this thief, and he will be sorry when I do."

BASIL AWAKENED to a din of clanging metal mixed with shrill, high-pitched screams emanating from the direction of the barn. Chickens squawked and clucked. Basil instantly threw back his bedcovers and bolted for the door of his room.

"I got him! Mother, I got him! I have caught the bandit!"

Basil did not even bother to put on his breeches or shoes. He grabbed his hunting gun from its resting place beside the door and ran as fast as he could down the stairs. Seconds later he jumped, barefoot, off of the back steps and darted toward the barn. He saw a floundering lump of humanity on the ground just outside the door of the chicken house. The fellow was wrapped with a web of rope and string. About a dozen tin pails and bowls, each tied to the end of one of the ropes or strings, clanged noisily against the ground.

Basil cocked his musket and aimed it at the thief. "Stop right there! Let me see your hands! I swear, I will shoot you!"

"Please don't shoot, Mister!" whined a high-pitched voice from inside the tangled web. "I ain't got no gun!" Two small, pale hands thrust upward through the tangled ropes into the cool night air. The frightened, dirty face of a small lad shone through the netting.

It was the voice of a child! Basil was confused. He had no expectations that a child would be guilty of stealing his chickens. He did not quite know what to do.

Basil's mother and sister each appeared on the back porch, both of them carrying a beeswax candle on a pewter stand.

His mother barked, "Put that gun away, Basil! It is just a little boy!"

Basil immediately lowered the weapon and released the flintlock hammer from its cocked position. He marched over to the entangled child and gave him a swift kick.

"Ouch!" moaned the culprit. "Why did you have to go and do that?"

"Because you are a stinking little thief, that's why!"

"That is quite enough, Basil!" Elizabeth declared. "Cut the child loose and bring him into the kitchen."

THE BOY practically inhaled the half-loaf of bread that Martha sat before him. He washed it down with copious amounts of fresh milk. The child was a pitiful sight, indeed. He wore neither stockings nor shoes. His threadbare linen breeches had not been functioning pants for quite some time. They hung in tatters and shreds from his skinny hips. He wore a dark blue shirt with one entire sleeve missing. A tangled mass of filthy, matted hair stuck out haphazardly from his hatless head.

"What is your name, Boy?" inquired Elizabeth. "You do not look familiar to me. Is your family near?"

The boy kept eating, intentionally ignoring Elizabeth's

questions.

"What is your mother's name?"

Again, the lad ignored the inquisitive woman. He looked away from members of the Billingsley family and stared at the window and door. It was clear that the little thief was attempting to discern a possible route of escape.

Basil, now fully clothed and wearing his leather boots, kicked the lad harshly in the shin. "Answer her questions!"

The little boy responded with almost invisible speed. He jumped from the chair and lunged at Basil. He buried his knee in the older boy's belly and began to claw at his eyes. Basil was caught off-guard at first, but quickly recovered and tossed the boy off of his lap onto the rough wood floor. Quick as a flash, the little boy darted for the door. Basil caught him from behind just as his right hand was removing the locking latch.

"I have had just about enough of you!" Basil screamed. He grabbed the boy by the hair on the back of his head and slammed his forehead against the heavy wood door. The blow stunned and temporarily immobilized the child.

"Basil!" screeched Elizabeth. "Is that really necessary?"

"Mother, did you not see what he just did? He is not only a thief. He is a wild animal, I tell you!"

The boy attempted to spin around and loosen himself from Basil's grip. The older boy merely tightened his hold on the lad.

"Son, we mean you no harm," Elizabeth promised. "We just want to find out where you are from and why you are stealing from us."

"Enough of this talk!" Basil chirped. "Martha, help me get him to the necessary house. We will lock him in there and I will go and fetch the sheriff."

The boy's eyes widened with fear. "No! Please! Don't lock me up! And please, don't call the sheriff!"

The wild little boy stared pleadingly at Elizabeth. She stared back, somewhat suspicious.

"If Basil releases you, do you promise to sit down and behave?"

"Yes ma'am."

"And no more running for the door."

"As you wish, ma'am."

Her eyes narrowed. "Because, if you try that one more time, I shall turn you over to the sheriff."

The little boy nodded hesitantly. "I understand."

"Good," Elizabeth barked. "Now, sit down in that chair, show some respect, and tell me what I wish to know. Otherwise, I will be forced to summon the authorities."

"The who?" inquired the boy, confused.

"The authorities ... the constable."

The boy still looked confused.

"She's talking about the sheriff, you stinky little thief!" growled Basil. "Now, sit down, and do as you are told!"

Basil loosened his grip and escorted the boy to the chair where he had previously been sitting. He obediently plopped down onto the slick wood seat.

Elizabeth pulled up a chair of her own and sat down in front of him. She stared at him for a short while. The silence was most uncomfortable.

"Do you have anything else to eat?" the boy asked hopefully, interrupting the silence.

"Like a little chicken, perhaps?" Basil responded sarcastically. "We are running a bit low these days, I'm afraid."

Elizabeth exhaled angrily. "You will remain silent, Basil, and allow me to speak to the boy."

Basil's chin dropped in shame. "Yes, Mother."

Elizabeth turned her attention to the strange child. "First, let us begin with something simple. How old are you?"

"I am nine years old. But I will be ten in July."

"It is already August," Basil grunted angrily.

"Well ... I guess I'm ten, then!" the boy barked rebelliously.

The little fellow stuck out his tongue at Basil. The older boy smirked and looked away. He did not want to interfere with his mother's interrogation.

"And what is your name?" Elizabeth continued.

The boy glanced at her, took a deep, resolute breath, and exhaled, "Oliver Denkins."

"Denkins?" she echoed. "I am not familiar with that name. Are you from the northern part of the county? Who is your father?"

"I ain't from 'round here," the boy responded curtly.

"Oh? Where are you from, then?"

Oliver hesitated for a moment and stared into the eyes of the woman seated in front of him. She had a kindly face. He decided that he liked this woman. He felt that he could trust her.

"I'm from Wilkes County."

"Where, on earth, is that? I have never heard of it," Martha declared from her seat in a distant corner of the room.

"Georgia."

Elizabeth gasped. "Georgia? Why ... that's a hundred and fifty miles from here! How, on earth, did you come to be in Guilford County?"

"We've been wandering for a while now, and just kind of stumbled onto the place."

"We?" Elizabeth asked quickly. "Are your parents

with you?"

The boy's countenance fell. He slapped his leg and muttered what sounded like a curse under his breath. He had clearly given away a bit of information that he had no intention of sharing.

"Who else is with you, Oliver?" Elizabeth demanded.

The boy responded with almost a whisper. "My sister ... Anna."

"Oh, so you have a sister? Is she older than you?"

Oliver shook his head in the negative. Elizabeth's eyes widened with surprise.

"Oliver, how old is Anna?"

"She's five, I think."

Martha gasped and rose from her chair. She ran to her mother and placed her hand on her shoulder. The two women stared at one another in shock.

"Where is Anna?" Martha demanded. "Is she safe? Is she hurt?"

"She's fine. I left her back at the cave."

"The cave?" shrieked Martha. "You left a little baby girl alone in a cave?" Her face flushed red in disbelief.

Oliver shrugged. "Of course. It is where we sleep every night. I never leave to go hunting until she's asleep."

"You mean to go and do some stealing," Basil remarked in anger. Clearly, Basil was not moved by the boy's story.

Elizabeth slapped her son on the arm. He bit his lip and leaned silently back in his chair. He failed to see the point in all of the questioning. He simply wanted to give the boy over to the sheriff and be rid of the little stinker.

"Where are your parents, Oliver?" Elizabeth asked quietly, kindly.

The boy hesitated for a moment, and took a deep breath. "They are dead, ma'am."

A reverent silence filled the room. Elizabeth leaned in closer and took the boy's hands in her own.

"How did it happen, Oliver? Did they die on the journey?"

A tear formed in the lad's eye. He shook his head. "No ma'am. Men came to our cabin and killed my Papa. They strung him up in a tree. Mama hid us in the smokehouse. I watched everything through a crack between the logs. The men took Mama and hauled her off into the woods toward town. I heard her scream once." The tear swelled until it was huge and then cut a path downward through the dirt of his filthy cheek. "I never saw her again after that."

"Who were they, Oliver? Indians? Bandits?"

"No, ma'am. They were Tories. There was one man with them who wore a red coat."

"Was your papa in the militia?"

The child nodded and wiped a trickle of tear-induced snot from his red nose.

"Did you go to other family members for help? Your grandparents, or an aunt or uncle?"

Oliver shook his head once again. "We didn't have nobody else. It was just us. The closest house was about a mile away. We went there, but them folks was all hangin' from trees, too. Even the children."

Martha covered her face with her hands and wept.

Elizabeth squeezed his hands tightly. "How long ago did this happen, Oliver?"

"It was right after Christmas."

"Eight months ago?" she shouted in disbelief. "And the two of you have been alone and wandering all this time?"

The boy nodded. Elizabeth cast a quick glance at Basil. Silent tears crawled down both of his cheeks. The angry youth had discovered that he and this homeless child had much more in common than he ever could have imagined. Elizabeth smiled knowingly at Basil and then turned her attention back to the boy.

"Oliver, I want you to lead Basil to your cave. You will take a horse, and you will bring Anna back to our house. I will not have you two youngsters spending any more nights in dark, damp caves." She stared at her son. "Isn't that right, Basil."

Her son, his hard heart suddenly softened by the plight of the two children, nodded in agreement. He swallowed hard and cleared his throat. "Yes, Mother. I will most certainly fetch her back."

"Well, then, boys ... be on your way. Take a blanket for the little girl. And go quickly. It will be dawn in a couple of hours."

"Yes, Mother," responded Basil, rising to his feet. "Come along, Oliver."

Basil's entire tone had changed. He politely escorted the boy to the door and pulled the latch. Before leaving, he looked back at his mother. She smiled and winked. Basil grinned broadly, wiped his cheeks, and then closed the door silently behind him.

∾

Three Hours Later

ELIZABETH, Martha, and Basil Billingsley sipped from their cups of steaming hot tea as they stared at the two children. The little ones were sleeping soundly in one of the empty beds in Basil's room. The soft light of dawn was just beginning to bathe the room with its purple-pink glow.

"How long will they sleep, do you reckon?" asked Basil.

"There is no way to tell," his mother responded, shaking her head. "I cannot even fathom how two little children have managed to survive in the wilderness, on their own, for all of these months."

"And through the winter, no less," added Basil, with a measure of admiration.

"Well, whenever they do wake up, they are both getting baths. That much I do know!" declared Elizabeth. "And we shall have to wash those bedcovers immediately. The poor little wretches are filthy."

"They probably have the itch," Basil commented matter-of-factly. "And all manner of bugs and bites."

Elizabeth nodded. "No doubt, that is true."

"Are we keeping them, Mother?" Martha inquired bluntly, changing the subject.

Elizabeth sighed. "They are not stray cats, my dear."

"I know, Mother ... but you know what I mean. We cannot very well turn them back out into the woods, can we?"

"No, I do not suppose we can do that." She breathed deeply and pondered the situation. "We must look out for their well-being. It is the Christian thing to do. It is what Papa would do."

"So, then, we *are* keeping them?" Martha asked again, wishfully.

All three of them continued to stare at the sleeping children.

Elizabeth took a sip of her tea. "Yes, Martha. Of course, we are keeping them."

Martha squealed quietly from excitement. Basil grinned, wrapped his arm around his mother's shoulders, and hugged her tightly against his side.

8

BIG BROTHER

The Denkins children slept soundly until noon. After providing each of them with a bowl full of hot porridge, Elizabeth extended a formal invitation for them to remain for as long as they liked. Oliver accepted somewhat reservedly. Anna cheered with glee.

But all the cheering stopped when Elizabeth informed them of their impending baths.

It was quite the ordeal. It took the entire afternoon and three tubs of hot water to remove eight months of untouched dirt and grime. Basil shook his head in disbelief each time he emptied the tub of its thick, muddy water.

Beneath the caked-on dirt the Billingsleys were shocked to discovered that the children had heads full of yellow-blonde hair. Before the baths, their hair had appeared to be a light shade of brown. Their golden locks were a matted, gnarled mess. Martha managed to detangle and make some progress with Anna's hair. After an hour of combing and the resulting whining and screaming, Elizabeth finally gave up on trying to fix Oliver's rather lengthy hair. She sheared it off short, beneath all the knots and tangles.

Basil burned the clothing that the children had worn, without changing, for eight months ... not that there was much left to burn. He wanted to make sure that he exterminated the ticks, fleas, and other little critters that surely inhabited the filthy garments. He was actually afraid to touch the clothes. He used long sticks to remove them to the fire pit behind the barn.

Elizabeth and Martha took great pleasure in digging out old pieces of children's clothing from the trunks in the attic and altering them to fit the orphans. The combined wardrobes of all of the Billingsley children provided plenty of items to choose from. It took very little time to locate breeches, shirts, and weskits for Oliver. They discovered an entire box of petticoats and short gowns that fit little Anna perfectly.

Anna latched onto Martha almost immediately, and Martha fell hopelessly in love with the quiet little girl. She doted over the child, dressing her up and caring for her as if she were a living doll. Martha saw to her every need, both physical and emotional. When Anna admired Martha's prized rag doll that rested on a shelf in Martha's room, the young woman immediately surrendered it to the excited and grateful child.

The children were in surprisingly good health. Basil attributed their relative well-being to Oliver's keen skills at thievery. But he knew full-well that simply stealing food from farms had not been the only thing that kept the children alive all these months. The lad had somehow managed to keep them both sheltered and warm. And, until last night, he had not been caught! That, to Basil, was the most amazing thing. Surely, Oliver Denkins was one clever and resourceful little boy.

Anna had two pretty serious wounds on one of her

legs. It appeared that something sharp ... perhaps a stick ... had punctured the soft flesh in her right thigh. Elizabeth helped Martha wash and clean the painful wounds. Elizabeth bathed them with a mixture of apple cider vinegar and water, and then wrapped them with clean bandages.

She declared with absolute confidence, "My vinegar should have those cuts healed up nicely in a day or two!"

Throughout the entire ordeal of cleansing and clothing the children, the two little ones never stopped eating. It was as if their bodies were empty caverns of hunger that could not be filled. They ate every morsel that the women placed in front of them ... and always asked for more. It took almost two days of non-stop eating before the children finally appeared satisfied.

By the third day after their adoption into the Billingsley home, Oliver Denkins had become Basil's "shadow." The lad followed the older boy's every step. He helped Basil with the livestock in the barn. He walked with him to run errands in town. He excitedly accompanied Basil on hunting expeditions in the forests around Guilford Courthouse. If Basil washed his hands, Oliver did the same. If Basil ate, then Olive ate. If Basil went to the necessary house, Oliver followed right behind him.

The little boy, who had been so quiet and reserved on the night that he was captured, turned out to be quite the talker. He chattered constantly, and peppered Basil with one question after another. It seemed clear that the boy was starved, not just for information, but for the presence of a grown man in his life. Basil was exactly the companion that he longed for.

Basil Billingsley had never had an opportunity to teach or guide anyone. He had always been, "Little Brother."

Indeed, he had never been anyone's "big brother" before. He discovered that he liked the role very much.

$$\sim$$

August 30, 1780

"So ... Samuel is your oldest brother?" asked a confused Oliver. He angled his hoe in order to chop the tall weed that grew beside a stalk of corn.

"Yes. Then James and John," answered Basil. "They are all married and have families of their own." Basil, too, was hoeing the sweet corn in the garden. He grinned at the inquisitive little boy.

"But I still haven't met any of them, yet."

"Correct. They are all in the militia service right now. However, I expect that they shall return in a week or two. Things have been quiet around our part of North Carolina. The British seem to be bogged down in the south."

Oliver nodded. "And Henry is the fellow at the farm ... the one with the busted leg, right?"

"Right. Henry is not married, yet. He is the real farmer of the family. I suppose he is the only one who paid attention to Papa for all those years. I doubt that we would eat very well without him."

"How did he hurt his leg?" Oliver inquired.

Basil stopped and leaned against the handle of his hoe. "It happened on the night that the men attacked our house and hanged Papa." He stared grimly at the little boy.

Oliver nodded his understanding. "So, he helped fight the bad men?"

"Yes, Oliver, he did. We all did."

Oliver's eyes widened with admiration. "You, too?"

Basil nodded. "Me, too. Or, at least, I tried. I was scared out of my mind. I rode into the middle of the shootout, took just one shot with my brother's huge pistol, and then promptly tumbled off of my horse. I got the wind knocked out of me, so I just lay still and waited until it was all over."

Oliver giggled. But, after a moment, his face became cloudy and grim. "Well, at least you tried. I didn't even try to save my papa." He chopped angrily at the weeds.

Basil stopped his work immediately and knelt beside the lad. Oliver stopped swinging his hoe. Basil placed a reassuring hand on the little boy's shoulder.

"Oliver, I am certain that there was nothing you could have done." He paused. "And I am amazed at how you escaped and took such good care of your sister all those many months. I do not think that I could have done as well as you did. I am impressed ... and most proud of you. All of us are."

Oliver smiled uncomfortably and then quickly resumed his work. Basil detected the glimmer of a tear in his left eye. He clearly wanted to change the emotional subject.

"And you have how many sisters, again?"

Basil resumed his chopping, as well. "Just three. Elizabeth and Cleary are both married and on their own. You know Martha, of course."

Oliver grinned. "She sure likes Anna!"

"She loves Anna," agreed Basil. "She makes over her like she was her very own child. I think it is good for Martha to have someone to take care of."

"And she sure is pretty," remarked Oliver. He tilted his head slightly and whistled.

"Who? Martha?"

Oliver nodded and grinned mischievously.

"Do you really think so?" asked Basil, a bit surprised that a little boy would say such a thing.

"Ain't no doubt!" he chirped. "She's the prettiest girl I ever saw."

"I do not suppose I have ever noticed."

Oliver giggled once again. Basil really enjoyed the sound of his high-pitched laugh.

Oliver continued his questions. "And you have one other brother? His name is Walter, right?"

"Yes. He is just a few years older than me. We grew up together. We are very close."

"Where is Walter now?" Oliver asked innocently.

Basil stopped hoeing, once again. He stared in the distance toward the field to their south. He exhaled deeply. "I do not know where he is, Oliver. The army took him, and we have not heard from him for quite some time." He paused. "I just hope he is still alive."

Oliver could see that Basil was deeply concerned about Walter. He wanted to encourage the older boy.

"Basil, you're so lucky. You have all these brothers." He poked his lips out slightly. "I've never even had one brother in my whole life."

Walter reached down and tapped the brim of the lad's floppy hat so that it hung down over his face. "Well, you do now, you little chicken thief." He grinned warmly.

Oliver righted his hat, smiled broadly, and continued to slash weeds with his hoe.

∼

"MOTHER, I hope that the pot is full! You have two hungry farm workers on your hands!"

Basil and Oliver burst into the parlor to find Elizabeth

and Martha locked in a tearful embrace. Anna was playing quietly with two dolls in the light of the front window.

Basil blurted, "Mother, what is wrong? Why are you two crying?"

Elizabeth rose to her feet. "Oh, my dear boy! Nothing is wrong. In fact, we have received the most wonderful news! Walter is alive!"

"What? How do you know? What news have you received?"

She offered him a worn, crumpled letter. "This came less than an hour ago. It is from Abigail."

Basil's eyes opened wide with shock. It had been months since they received word from Walter. Basil had secretly feared that his brother was injured or dead. He grabbed the letter from his mother's hands and quickly scanned its words. His lips moved rapidly as he read each line.

Basil glanced at his mother, confused. "Walter is in prison in South Carolina?"

"A prison of war, my dear. He was captured by Tories many weeks ago."

Basil shook his head grimly. "The Redcoats do not take very good care of their prisoners."

Elizabeth nodded knowingly. "And neither the Continental Army nor the Congress offer any provisions for our prisoners. It is a crime, in my opinion."

Basil nodded his agreement and continued to read. "Holy thunder! Walter was in a battle? That lucky dog!" He grinned broadly, but then his smile quickly converted to a frown. "But Gabriel Tate is dead."

"Yes. It is tragic. That boy was a jester and a fool, but I never harbored any ill will against him. My heart breaks for his parents. I must inform them immediately. I will go to their home after tea."

"And I will accompany you, Mother," Basil promised.

"We all will!" added Martha.

Basil scanned the letter again. "I wonder how Abigail found out where Walter was imprisoned."

Elizabeth shrugged. "I do not know. The prison is in Camden, where the Hamer family lives. Perhaps her father had a reason to go there."

"I don't suppose that it matters." Basil glanced at the upper right corner of the letter. "This date is almost a month ago. It took that long for a letter to travel from Camden?"

"Yes, Son. Camden is under British control. By some miracle, Mr. Hamer managed to get the letter smuggled out of Camden by sending it through a personal contact in Charlestown. Apparently, it then traveled by sea through the port at Jamestown. A postal rider carried it overland to us, and delivered it today."

"That was quite a roundabout, wandering route for such a tiny little letter," mumbled Basil.

His mother sighed. "Indeed. It is a miracle, in my opinion. The entire set of circumstances is miraculous."

Basil smiled and took his mother by the hand. "It is truly remarkable, I agree. So ... Walter is alive. What must we do now?"

Elizabeth's chin dropped to her chest. "There is nothing practical that we can do, Basil. Not from such a great distance. But we must pray, both for Walter and for the Hamer family."

"Of course, Mother. We shall pray that Walter will return to us very soon."

"With his lovely bride by his side," added Martha, smiling broadly.

The three of them leaned forward in a loving embrace.

The sound of a little boy clearing his throat interrupted their family moment.

Oliver declared, "If Walter is not going to be back here in the next little bit, do you reckon we could go ahead and have some supper? I'm near-on starved."

Everyone in the parlor burst into joyous laughter.

PART III

THE WAR OUTSIDE OUR WINDOW - 1781

9

THE PATRIOTS ARRIVE

March 13, 1781

"Just a little bit more!" encouraged Oliver from his position beneath the wagon.

Basil gave the wheel a slight turn to the right.

"Perfect!" exclaimed Oliver. "Now, hold it right there."

The wood vibrated against Basil's hands as Oliver tapped a pin into place. The high-pitched pinging of his hammer against the iron pin echoed from beneath the rig.

The boys were completing the installation of the wagon's new front axle. The complicated iron and wood contraption had to be replaced after the original one broke during a recent trip to Salisbury. The Quaker blacksmith and carpenter in New Market had worked together to produce an excellent new axle, much superior to the original. However, the piece of equipment had been quite costly. The blacksmith required a payment in trade of two calves. Thankfully, the small herd of heifers on the Billingsley farm had birthed sixteen calves during the late winter. Because of the importance of a functional wagon, Henry reluctantly parted with two of the young beef critters.

"Almost done!" Oliver proclaimed excitedly. He gave the steel pin two more hard strikes. "That should do it!"

Basil released his grip on the wheel as Oliver extracted himself from beneath the front axle of the wagon.

"Did everything look nice and tight under there?"

Oliver nodded. "It was a perfect fit. I rubbed some of that grease on the tip of the pin. Once I got it started, it was no problem, at all. It went right into place."

"Good job," Basil declared, patting the boy on the shoulder. "Now, let us go and test it out. We can deliver our weekly load of wood to the bakery." He grinned and winked at the younger boy. "Mrs. McGregor always makes her apple fried pies on Tuesday."

"Let's get that wood loaded!" Oliver declared happily.

The boys enjoyed their regular deliveries of firewood to the bakery in Guilford. Their little enterprise gave Basil and Oliver the opportunity to earn some extra income and provisions for the family. Plus, each trip always resulted in some special treats. Oliver adored how Mrs. McGregor always rewarded them with a couple of morsels of sweet breads, pies, or biscuits. Basil loved how Miss Ellen McGregor, the baker's handsome, red-haired, thirteen-year-old daughter always seemed to stare and smile at him. He was smitten by the pretty young girl, and eagerly anticipated his weekly deliveries of firewood to her family's business. He would deliver wood on a daily basis, if he could, in order to catch a glimpse of Ellen.

The boys tossed their tools and gear into the storage box behind the seat and quickly hooked up the team of horses to the wagon. Within seconds they were bouncing along the bumpy trail that led to the pile of split firewood behind

John's house. They topped a small rise bordered by a large field to the west. It was the Billingsley family's hayfield, located in the center of their vast acreage.

The sight that greeted them in that hayfield took their breath away. The open ground was filled with hundreds of white tents. Dozens of horses grazed among the high grasses to the north. Large formations of soldiers marched to and fro around the edges of the field. Basil pulled back on the reins and cooed at the horses to stop.

"What the devil is going on?" wailed Oliver. "Where did all those soldiers come from?"

Basil stared worriedly at the field. "I do not know. But we shall find out."

He clucked at the horses and urged them down the hill toward the encampment. About fifty yards from the first cluster of tents, they encountered four soldiers manning a checkpoint on the wagon trail. Each of the men were dressed in brightly-colored blue and red Continental Army uniforms. Two of the men blocked the road. The other two approached the wagon.

"Can I help you boys?" inquired one of the soldiers. He was young, no more than eighteen or nineteen years old.

"Perhaps," responded Basil. "You can tell me what the devil is going on, and why you people are fouling up my family's hayfield."

The soldier glanced suspiciously over his shoulder at his compatriots. "This is your family's land?"

"That is what I said," responded Basil curtly.

"It is my understanding that this land is owned by one of the officers in a local militia regiment ... a captain. He is the reason that we are encamped here."

"A captain? Was it James Billingsley?"

"I could not say," the soldier responded. "I never heard his name ... only his rank."

Basil nodded. It must have been his big brother, James. He was the only officer from amongst the militia-serving Billingsley brothers.

Basil glanced toward the encampment. "Where are you fellows from, Sergeant? I've never seen an actual Continental uniform before."

The man seemed impressed that Basil recognized his rank. "We're with the 1st Virginia Regiment, Captain John Anderson's Company. But the men in this field are from all over. Most are from the Carolinas and Virginia. There are a few Marylanders, and a handful of stragglers from Delaware. But, we are all here for the same reason ... to fight the British. We are waiting for the county militias from throughout this region to join us."

"Is there going to be a fight around here?" questioned Oliver, eyes opened wide with awe. His entire face betrayed his fascination with the military spectacle on display in front of him.

"I cannot say, young man," the soldier responded, smiling. "All I can report is that it will be in your best interest to return to your home. Please ... for your own safety."

"I have brothers in the Rowan and Randolph County Regiments," Basil declared, ignoring the soldiers polite request for them to leave.

"Both regiments have men encamped here," the soldier responded flatly.

Basil nodded. "My other brother, Walter, is with the Virginia Regulars. He was in a fight at the Waxhaws Meeting House down in South Carolina. Last we heard, he was in a British prison down in Camden."

"I am sorry to hear that," commented the Virginian. He

glanced at the ground. "Well, gents, I sincerely hate to be rude, but we really do need you to be on your way. We must keep this roadway open for military traffic."

Basil sighed and lifted up the reins. "Of course. I understand."

He was just about to give the leather straps a tug when he heard a familiar voice from the tree-line to their left.

"Basil? Oliver? What are you boys doing here?" It was Captain James Billingsley. He was sitting on horseback, and leading a squad of eight mounted soldiers.

Basil waved subtly at his brother. Oliver stood up on the wagon seat and waved excitedly. James grinned, turned and said something to his men, and then guided his horse toward Basil's wagon. His men trotted toward the encampment and quickly disappeared into the sea of tents.

"What is your identity, sir?" inquired the sergeant at the checkpoint.

"Captain James Billingsley, Rowan County Regiment. You are standing in my field."

"Your field?" the man asked incredulously.

"Yes. My field. I own it. This is my farm."

The sergeant nodded his understanding. "And you know these lads?"

James grinned. "Indeed, I do. They are my kin. You can let them through, Sergeant. They shall dine with me tonight."

"Mother will be sick with worry," responded Basil. "We should probably go on home."

James waved his hand dismissively. "Do not worry about that. I will send a runner with a message for mother. You boys will be in my capable hands." He turned to the sergeant. "Make way, Sergeant."

"As you wish, Captain." The sergeant smiled and waved the boys forward. "Enjoy your evening, gentlemen."

James turned his horse and headed toward the northern end of the encampment.

Basil reached up and tipped his black cocked hat respectfully toward the sergeant. "Thank you, sir. And thank you for your service to our nation."

The sergeant smiled broadly and then gave one of Basil's horses a quick slap on the rump. The animal gave a lurch, and then both horses trotted forward, pulling the empty wagon into the army camp.

BASIL AND OLIVER reclined against a log. Each held an empty bowl in his hand. Their bellies were stuffed with hot stew and fresh bread. James sat on a small stool on the opposite side of the campfire and sipped hot tea from a tin tankard. He simultaneously puffed on a short tobacco pipe made of clay.

"James, do you really think there will be a fight near us?" inquired Basil.

His older brother nodded grimly. "I have no doubt. General Greene has already selected the ground. It is a crossroad about a mile west of Guilford. He is trying to lure Cornwallis to the location."

"General Lord Cornwallis?" blurted Oliver. "From Charlestown?"

James took another sip of his steaming tea. "He has been out of Charlestown for quite some time now. After he got whipped at the Battle of Cowpens down in South Carolina, he chased our forces all the way to the Dan River. But General Greene managed to give him the slip. Now, Cornwallis is far from his home territory in South Carolina. His men are tired and running low on supplies. They are ripe for the picking."

"So, then ... Cornwallis is near?" asked Oliver fearfully.

James grunted and nodded. "He is encamped about ten miles to the east. Our scouts say that he is heading this way."

There was a long moment of silence. Basil finally broke it with a declaration. "Well, then, I shall join your regiment immediately, James. Where do I sign, Captain?"

James puffed his pipe and shook his head vigorously. "You will do no such thing. You must take care of our mother. And, besides, I have other matters that require your attention."

"Like what supposing?" Basil hissed angrily. He did not like for James to tell him what to do. And he certainly did not like for him to forbid his volunteering for the militia.

James glanced around to ensure that no one was listening to their conversation. "Boys, this valley is going to be crawling with men. I expect that we will have over 4,000 encamped here by tomorrow. The British could have twice as many."

"So?" asked Basil, confused.

"So ... they are all going to be foraging the countryside for food. Can you imagine? 8,000 to 10,000 men ... and all of them looking for something to eat?"

Basil suddenly understood. He exclaimed, "Our livestock!"

"Yes," responded James. "The few livestock we have left are in jeopardy. I have already given a half-dozen heifers to the cause. But that was nowhere near enough to meet the needs of this army. The beef lasted only one day. If we are not careful, we could lose our entire herd. I am quite certain that our armies would be honorable and provide reimbursement. But the British most certainly would not. They are desperate. They will take whatever they need."

Basil's mind reeled at the thought of losing all of their cows. "That's over two hundred head, James!" he exclaimed. He pondered the notion. "Surely, they will clean out our sheep and goats, as well."

"And chickens!" added Oliver.

James nodded. "And they will empty out every smoke-house, cellar, and corn crib in this region." He spat on the ground. "Our people will get mighty hungry before the crops are ready in the fall."

"If the armies do not simply destroy all of the planted fields," Basil added.

"Exactly," declared James. "If the crops are wiped out, and the livestock are all slaughtered and eaten, there will be starvation and suffering in the coming winter. We simply cannot allow it to happen to our family."

"What would you have us to do?" asked Basil.

"You must hide all of our stores and livestock. I suggest you begin at first light tomorrow." He paused and took another sip of his tea. "The battle will be upon us soon."

"How soon?" inquired Oliver.

"Two days. Three at most."

Oliver's eyes grew wide. He glanced at the village of linen tents that surrounded him. All throughout the encampment, men were eating, smoking their pipes, talking, and laughing. Somewhere in the distance he heard the sound of a violin playing a mournful tune. There was peace and comfort in the comfortable camp. He could scarcely believe that these relaxed, happy men would soon be called upon to march into battle.

"Where will we put everything?" inquired Basil.

James shrugged his shoulders. "All of our stores need to

be hidden underground. I suppose you might have to dig out a hide."

"What about a cave?" asked Oliver.

James shook his head. "We don't have any caves on our land."

"I'm not talking about the Billingsley land. I'm talking about my cave," Oliver answered excitedly. "Sissy and I hid out there for weeks and no one found us. I doubt anyone even knows it is there ... except for some Indians, maybe."

James glanced at Basil. "Where is this cave?"

"About a half-mile west of town, deep in the woods. It's up in a draw, near the top of a hill. Oliver is right. I doubt anyone else has ever spotted it before. It is concealed and not near any cabins or houses. The opening is small ... barely large enough for a man to squeeze through. I don't even know how Oliver found it." He punched the boy playfully in his shoulder.

"Is there enough room for storage?" asked James.

Oliver nodded convincingly. "The entrance is small, and there is a narrow walkway down deeper into the hill, but it opens up into a big room."

James raised one eyebrow. "How big?"

"At least a twenty-foot circle. Maybe a little bigger than that."

James pondered the boy's description. "It definitely sounds like it is large enough." He took a deep breath. "I want you boys to work with Henry tomorrow and collect all of the foodstuffs, weapons, powder ... anything that an army might take ... and haul it by wagon to that cave."

"It will take a couple of trips," cautioned Basil.

"As well I know it," exhaled James. "Once you are finished with all of the supplies, I want you to hide our livestock. Start with all of our horses and beef cattle. Then, work your way down to the sheep, pigs, and goats."

"Where do we take them?" asked Basil.

"As far south on our land as you can. Do you remember that little meadow surrounded by the rock walls?"

Basil nodded. "Yes! I have not been there in a couple of years. But, it is a perfect spot! There is only one way in and out, through that tight little draw."

"Indeed," responded James. "And there is even water there. A spring spills out of the western wall and feeds a small puddle in the rock beneath. It is not much water, but it should suffice for a few days."

"We can put up a small fence at the mouth of the draw," added Basil.

James shook his head. "No, put your fence in deeper toward the meadow. But, be sure to cut some small saplings and brush to conceal the opening of the draw. Then, go back each morning and cut fresh cover for the spot ... make sure everything stays nice and green. Hopefully, by week's end, this will all be over and you boys can go and fetch the animals home."

Basil smiled at his brother. "It is a good plan, James."

"I know it is, Little Brother. Now, you and this little chicken thief need to go and get it done."

Oliver grinned broadly and his face flushed red.

Basil sat his empty bowl on a rock beside the fire and stood. "We will take care of everything, James. You can count on us." He reached out his hand to his brother. James shook his hand and then pulled Basil toward him and gave him a huge hug. Oliver darted toward them and inserted himself into the brotherly embrace. James chuckled with joy at the lad.

"I know I can count on you, Little Brother." He released

both boys from his embrace. "I want you two to take care of Mother and the girls. And be sure to tell Mother that I am thinking of her."

"We will. Should we tell your wife the same?" Basil teased.

"I shall do that myself. I am going to check on her tonight." He paused and looked sternly at Basil and Oliver. "I want you boys to be careful. If you catch sight of any Redcoats, just turn and run the other way. Do you understand?"

Both boys answered, "Yes, James."

"I am very serious. Do not give them any excuse to take you captive."

Basil stared solemnly into his brother's eyes. "We will do as you say. I promise."

"Good. Now, off with the both of you. Go and get some sleep. We all have a big day ahead of us tomorrow."

10

REDCOATS AND LIES

"What about that?" asked Basil as he wiped the sweat from his brow. "Does it look suspicious, at all?"

Both boys stared at the entrance to the hidden canyon in the hills. It was freshly-decorated with branches and freshly-cut saplings.

Oliver stared at the pile of brush and then broke into a wide grin. "It is perfect, Basil! It just looks like a small thicket. I cannot see any portion of the fence."

Basil stood back and admired their work. "Well, then ... I suppose that we are finished!"

"We are, indeed," affirmed Oliver. "Let us go and find some dinner. I am famished."

Basil did not respond verbally. He merely turned and walked toward their horses, which were tied to a tree at the edge of the woods.

Oliver and Basil had been working since dawn on the task that James had assigned them on the previous evening. They had, however, changed the order of things a bit. James had instructed them to move all of their foodstuffs and supplies to the cave first, and then relocate the livestock to the hideout. However, Basil thought it wise to move the animals in the cool of the morning. It was shaping up to be a warm day, and he preferred to get the hardest work done in the early morning.

It was a good decision. It had taken five hours to move all of the livestock from the family's fields and barns and into the safety of the small canyon in the hills. The noon hour was near. Both boys knew that Mrs. Billingsley would have a hot meal prepared for them when they arrived back home. Afterwards, they would get right to work on moving all of their stored food and provisions.

Basil fetched his rifle from its resting spot against a nearby tree and climbed nimbly onto his horse. Oliver followed his lead, grabbing his smaller .45 caliber flintlock.

"Let's cut cross-country and go over Nichols Creek," suggested Basil. "That way, we will avoid the army camp and any traffic on the roads. We can follow the tree line all the way to Guilford Courthouse."

Oliver nodded. "Just get me to that food!"

Basil smiled and popped the younger boy on the leg with his leather rein. "I swear, Oliver Denkins! I don't know where you put all of the food that you eat! You must store it in your leg, or something."

"I just work it off really fast." Oliver grinned.

Basil rolled his eyes. "C'mon. Mother is waiting."

Both boys spun guided their horses toward the north-west and rode along the edge of meadow, next to the tree line. It would be a short ride home. They had only about a mile and a half to travel.

The boys rode in silence, each of them lost in their thoughts. They had been traveling for only a few minutes when Oliver suddenly barked, "Into the trees! Quick!"

Oliver guided his horse into the woods with a sense of urgency.

Basil did not hesitate or question the younger boy's warning. He instantly followed suit. Once they were well-concealed in the shadows of the forest, both boys halted their horses and spun them around.

Basil whispered, "What is the matter? What did you see?"

"Redcoats!" Oliver hissed.

"What? Where?" Basil challenged.

"On the road to the east. I caught a glimpse of red. I think there were six or eight of them."

"On horseback?"

Oliver shook his head. "No. On foot, and headed toward town."

"Are you certain?"

"There is no mistaking those uniforms," retorted Oliver. "I've seen them before ... back home in Georgia." His face clouded from the painful memories.

Basil nodded. "I want to see for myself. Let's ease up to the edge of the woods for a look."

The boys snaked their horses through the thick woods and then crept up to the edge of the trees. They remained about ten feet inside the tree line, well into the shadows of the high canopy. They were careful to remain well-hidden behind the low brush that bordered the woods.

The sight of the crimson British made Basil's skin tingle. He could scarcely believe it. The enemy was upon them! The patrol of British soldiers marched steadily in the direction of Guilford.

"I count ten soldiers, Oliver. It is a patrol. They are, most likely, scouting out the town."

The younger boy did not respond. He never took his

eyes off of the British troops. He merely offered a slow, mesmerized nod.

"We have to get home, Oliver! There is no time to waste! The British could be invading the town at any moment. We have to get all of our stores out of the house and into the cave!"

"What about dinner?" wailed Oliver.

"Dinner will have to wait. If we don't get our supplies safely to that cave, there may not be any more dinners. Do you understand?"

"Yes, Basil."

"Let us go quickly, then. We shall head due west through the woods until we reach the river, then turn due north and work our way around town and come in from behind our house. Once we get there, we will not waste any time. I will hitch the wagon. You will need to get Mother, Martha, and Anna busy gathering and loading. We may only get one wagon load of goods before the British reach the town."

"Won't somebody try and stop them?" asked Oliver.

"Perhaps, if there are any militiamen nearby. But most of them are encamped with the Continentals to the northeast. I doubt that the constable or any of the men in town will resist. They are not exactly known for their bravery," Basil mocked. He took a deep breath. "We need to go!"

He spun his horse around and directed it toward the west, guiding it toward the darkness of the deep woods.

BASIL AND OLIVER rode into town from the north, along the Virginia highway. All of Guilford Courthouse was in an uproar. It was obvious that word of the approaching British soldiers had already reached the town. The entire populace was in a frenzy. It seemed that every house on Main Street was being emptied of its valuables. Families were feverishly loading horses and wagons with clothing, silverware, candle stands, furniture, and paintings.

Basil looked at Oliver and shook his head. Most of the people were acting impetuously and foolishly. Basil knew full-well that the British had no interest in looting homes for valuables. An army, so far from its supply depots in South Carolina, would need food, powder, and lead. The citizens of Guilford Courthouse would soon learn a very expensive and humbling lesson.

Elizabeth and Martha Billingsley were standing on the front porch when the boys arrived. Little Anna Denkins stood between them, confused by the frantic activity on the front lawns of the surrounding houses. Elizabeth breathed a sigh of relief when she saw the boys.

"Goodness sakes, Basil! I was worried sick that the British had taken you!"

Basil replied, "We are just fine, Mother. We saw them approaching the town, and stayed far away from them."

"Are the livestock safe?" his mother asked.

Basil nodded. "They will be fine for a few days. They have ample graze and water. We secured them in a small, steep-sided draw with a solid fence. It is concealed very well. I doubt anyone will stumble across it."

"What must we do now, Basil?" wailed his sister Martha. "Everyone else is taking all their valuables away and hiding them in the woods. Mary Swanson told me that the Redcoats are coming to plunder all of our belongings!"

"They are not being sensible," Basil replied as he climbed down from his horse. "The British are coming for supplies, not plunder. They are hungry, and lacking in basic necessities. We must gather all of our food stores, weapons, and ammunition. Oliver and I already have a hiding spot picked out."

"Where?" Elizabeth inquired.

"Oliver and Anna's cave. It is a perfect place to conceal everything."

She nodded. "That is, indeed, a good spot. How can we help?"

"I will go and hitch the team to the wagon. Meanwhile, I need all of you to begin gathering our foodstuffs on the back porch. Empty out the cellar ... every sack of flour and corn meal. Grab every jar of fruit and jam. I don't want the Lobsterbacks to get a single mouthful from this house." He turned to Oliver. "Ollie, I need you to get all of the meat from the smokehouse. Just drop it from the hooks and wrap it in cloth."

He turned to Martha. "Sister, I want you to get all of the chickens. There are two chicken cages in the barn. We only have the one rooster and about twenty layers left. They should all fit inside the cages. We'll load the chicken cages on top of the food."

Martha shook her head. "I'm scared of that rooster, Basil. I don't think I can catch it."

He rolled his eyes. "Well, then, just forget the rooster. But save the hens. We need the eggs. The British will simply kill and roast our egg-layers."

"Are you sure that we should take everything?" asked his mother.

"Most definitely. Keep just enough to cook supper tonight. We can always go and fetch some of the supplies, if we need to." Basil jumped down from his horse and tied it to the hitching rail. "We are wasting time. Let's get to work!"

The women disappeared into the house as Basil and

Oliver ran toward the barn. It took only a few minutes for Basil to prepare the wagon and park it behind the house.

They worked at a feverish pitch. The ladies brought the food out onto the back porch and placed it there for Basil to load in the wagon. He first lined the bottom of the rig with all of the heavy sacks of grain, flour, and meal. The jars and boxes of food came next, followed by all of the smoked meat. Oliver was loading the last of the guns, powder, and lead beneath the seat of the wagon as Basil secured the final cage full of chickens to the top of the pile. Somehow, almost miraculously, the family had managed to secure and load all of their food and supplies in less than thirty minutes.

Martha held her finger to her lips and hissed, "Listen! What is that?"

Everyone stood perfectly still and listened. There was shouting from the far end of town. They were distinctly British voices. Then came a frightened scream of a woman.

Basil jumped into the seat of the wagon. He barked, "Let's go, Oliver! They are here! We must make our escape!"

Oliver jumped into the passenger seat and held tightly to the side handle as Basil snapped the reins and yelled at the horses. The wagon lurched forward onto the narrow trail that led in the direction of the cave.

"Are you sure it is safe to go back now?" asked Oliver, his voice trembling slightly. "Those soldiers may still be there. And all of those people were yelling and screaming as we rode away ..." He was sitting on top of a rock and watching Basil unhitch the team of horses from the wagon.

"What kind of question is that, Ollie? Mama and the girls are back at the house. They are alone and unprotected.

We have to go back. They need us. I pray that they are unharmed."

Oliver's chin dropped to his chest. He was clearly afraid, and somewhat ashamed that he had not thought of the Billingsley women and his baby sister.

Sweat soaked Basil's back and hat. He was thoroughly exhausted from the day's work. They had been concealing animals and food since morning's first light. Nevertheless, as tired as he was, he continued to untie the leather straps that connected the horses to the wagon tongue. His plan was simple. They would leave the wagon concealed deep in the woods and then ride the horses back into town.

"So, why are we hiding the wagon way out here?" asked Oliver innocently.

Basil grunted, disgusted. He spat on the ground. "Those slimy Redcoats would likely take it if they had the chance. Remember, we saw them marching on foot into Guilford. No doubt, their plan was to commandeer a wagon and fill it with plundered supplies. They would have no other way to get their booty back to their encampment."

Oliver responded quietly, "Oh. I hadn't thought of that."

Basil pushed the wagon into a small draw between two large rocks and then concealed it with limbs and brush. He wiped the sweat from his brow with his floppy hat and stared, satisfied, at his work.

"That should do for now. I doubt anyone will be rambling around out here in these woods, anyhow. We can come back and get our wagon after the British are gone."

"When do you think that will be, Basil?"

"I am not sure. Soon, I hope." He winked at the younger boy. "Now, hop up on that bareback mare, and let us head toward home. We will enter town from the south and come in on Main Street. If we are stopped by the British and questioned, we will say that we were visiting James' house and checking on Ann. No more details than that."

Oliver nodded. "I will just let you do the talking."

"Good idea." Basil grinned. "Now, let's get moving. I'm famished!"

"Stop and dismount!" the Redcoat sergeant commanded as he stepped into the roadway. He held a heavy Brown Bess musket menacingly across his chest.

The fellow surprised and startled the boys. Oliver almost tumbled from the top of his horse. The boys had not seen the sentry as they rode into town. The fellow had concealed himself behind an outdoor toilet alongside the road.

The soldier frowned. "I say there, lads. Why are you so jumpy? You're up to no good, I'll wager." His British accent was thick.

"You scared us, that's all," Basil responded. "We don't often have soldiers leaping out from behind the necessary house."

The soldier glanced down the road behind them. "Where are you boys coming from, and what is your business in this town?"

"We live here," answered Basil. He pointed up the street. "That is our house on the left ... the big red-brick one."

The soldier glanced at the house and nodded. "What is your name?"

"Basil Billingsley. This is my little brother, Oliver."

"What were you doing outside the town?"

"I was not aware that there were any laws against traveling outside the boundaries of town," Basil retorted harshly. "What business is it of yours, anyway?"

The soldier sighed and frowned. "You are correct. There are no such laws. I am merely attempting to discover whether or not you are a threat to our patrol."

Basil smiled thinly. "We are unarmed, sir, and certainly no threat to you. We have merely been to the home of our brother, James. We wanted to check in on his wife and see if she needed anything."

The soldier eyed Basil suspiciously. "Why does the woman require your special attention? Where is your brother?"

"He is away on business. Ann and James have three small children. There were chores to be done. We hauled water, brought in firewood, and tidied up the barn. We were simply trying to be good brothers, that's all." Basil paused. "What are you soldiers doing here?"

"We are scouting ahead of the army and foraging for supplies."

"Supplies?" Basil queried.

"Food, mostly. Our stores are running low. We are also confiscating weapons and powder, whenever we can find them."

"Why weapons and powder?" Basil challenged.

The soldier snorted slightly. "We know that the rebel militia is operating in the area. We want to make sure we will not be shot in the back by some foolish farmers or peasants."

Basil was about to respond when Oliver's high-pitched voice interrupted the interrogation. "Can we go now, mister? We're hungry, and our mama is going to be mighty angry if we're late for supper." He stared impatiently at the soldier.

The Englishman, believing the boys to be honest, broke into a warm smile. He lowered his musket.

"Off you go, then. I wouldn't want lads as big as you getting a spanking tonight."

Basil nodded. "Thank you, sir."

The British soldier tipped his hat. "I wish you both a pleasant evening. We will be gone within the hour."

Basil and Oliver clucked at their horses and guided them past the checkpoint. Both boys were anxious to get home and check on their women-folk. They were equally as anxious to fill their bellies with a hot meal. They only hoped that the Redcoats had not stolen their supper.

11

THE BILLINGSLEY HOSPITAL

Mid-Morning - March 15, 1781

The Billingsleys, like most of the other families in Guilford Courthouse, stood stoically on their front porch. Some were brave enough to stand out on their lawns. The people of the village stared toward the north, in the direction of the freshly-plowed fields just outside the town limits. No one spoke. They were entirely too mesmerized to speak. Thousands of British troops marched across the field in perfect formation. Hundreds of green and red-clad soldiers on horseback rode on both sides of the immense army of foot-soldiers. It was an impressive, frightening sight.

"Where are they going?" asked Anna. Her tiny voice trembled with fright. She hugged her tiny rag doll close to her chest.

"They are going off to some battlefield," Mrs. Billingsley reassured her. "They have no interest in us. They are here to fight the Continental Army."

"Mother is right, Anna." Basil placed a reassuring hand

on her shoulder. "They are moving west of town. The Continental army and our North Carolina militia have been encamped on our farm to the southwest. They must have left during the night, and the British are pursuing them."

"But, will there be a battle close by?" the tiny girl responded, lip trembling.

Basil smiled and shook his head. "I do not believe so. They will probably travel several miles to the west. There is more open ground near New Market."

His confident words had just departed his lips when the thunderous roar of cannon fire erupted to the northwest, just beyond the borders of town. The concussion of the guns made the ground tremble and rattled the glass in the windows of their home. The Battle of Guilford Courthouse had begun.

Elizabeth Billingsley shot a concerned look at her son. "That was close, Basil."

Her son frowned. "I may have been mistaken."

Another loud barrage of cannon fire rocked the town. It shook the ground so hard that the dust in the street danced upward in tiny clouds and hovered above the ground.

Moments later a dozen British dragoons broke away from the immense army and rode into the town. The men dispersed and approached the homes along the street. Some of the nearby residents turned to flee to the safety of their houses.

One of the horse soldiers shouted, "We mean you no harm! Please, wait just a moment! We have an announcement for the entire village!"

The frightened citizens stopped and stared at the soldiers. The officer in charge moved to a position in the center of the street, right in front of the Billingsley house.

The man cleared his throat and declared, "His Excellency, General Lord Cornwallis, ordered us to visit this town to warn the citizens to stay inside their homes for the remainder of the day. There is to be a battle no more than a mile to the west of here. For your safety, please do not venture in the direction of the gunfire." He nodded. "That is all. You may return to your indoor activities."

The man turned and faced the Billingsley home. He urged his horse to take a few steps in the direction of the front porch. He tipped his hat to Elizabeth.

"Madam, I am Captain Blake Hollingsworth of His Majesty's British Legion. I am pleased to make your acquaintance." He locked eyes with the young and beautiful Martha Billingsley. He smiled broadly and tipped his hat again. "Young lady ..."

Elizabeth stepped in front of her daughter and nodded politely. "I am Elizabeth Billingsley. These are my children."

"And where is your husband, Madam? I must speak to him."

The widow bit her tongue and refrained from answering immediately. She decided that it would be best not to mention her family's history with the Tories.

"My husband is dead, Captain."

Quite unexpectedly, Basil spit on the ground in front of the captain's horse. He tilted his head toward the large oak tree near the captain's horse. "They hanged him in that tree beside you, Captain. Five years ago."

"Who hanged him?" the captain inquired, surprised.

"Some of your friends from South Carolina. Tory bandits, out to terrorize innocent folk. Most of them are buried together in the woods out behind our house." He spat again.

Basil stared at the man with a poisonous hatred. His emotion compelled him to fetch a pistol and shoot the enemy soldier, but wisdom enabled him to tame his feelings. He said nothing else. He merely stood fast and stared at the officer.

Captain Hollingsworth growled, "Indeed. How unfortunate for everyone involved."

Elizabeth interrupted their exchange. "How may I help you, Captain?"

Captain Hollingsworth surveyed the Billingsley house. "I need to inform you that we may have to make use of your home. It is the largest, and appears to be the sturdiest residence in the town."

"Use it for what?" demanded Basil.

"As a field hospital." The man shifted his weight in the saddle. "Before this day is over, we may very well need every home in this township in order to care for our wounded. But we shall start with yours."

"And we have no say in the matter?" Elizabeth asked incredulously.

"No, Madam. You do not. This is a matter of service to the Crown. Your obedience is expected. We will also require you to assist in rendering care."

Elizabeth objected, "We know nothing of such things, Captain. I will not have my children exposed to any more blood or violence."

The captain leaned forward in his saddle. "Mrs. Billingsley, if you refuse, we will simply remove you from your home. Do you understand?"

Elizabeth did not know what to say. She covered her mouth with her hand, too shocked to speak.

"Oh, we understand just fine!" Basil hissed.

"Very well, then. I shall inform our surgeons to occupy your residence immediately. Good day to you all."

Once again, the man tipped his hat. No one responded

to him, so he turned and guided his horse to toward the north. He and his men departed the township in a matter of seconds.

Martha tapped her mother on the shoulder. "What do we do now, Mother?"

"We do as they say, Martha. What choice do we have?"

~

Two Hours Later

ELIZABETH SHOUTED, "Hold his leg tightly! Do not let go!"

Basil strengthened his grip on the right leg of the wounded Redcoat. The man screamed and writhed in pain as he lay on the Billingsley family's dining table. The cannons continued to rumble at a frightening, deafening pace. Dust and plaster rained down from overhead, dislodged from the structure of the house by the repeated concussions.

The battle had been raging for almost an hour. It took only a scant few minutes after the first explosions of musket fire began for the first wounded soldiers to begin trickling in. As the pace of the fighting increased, so, too, did the flow of the wounded. For the time being, they were all British soldiers, but Basil was certain that there would be American Patriots amongst them before the day was done.

Basil was tired. He took a deep breath as he glanced at the carnage and confusion inside his home. At least two dozen men lay on the floors throughout the first floor. Several others, treated within the first hour, had been evacuated to the barn. The more critical patients were upstairs in the Billingsley family's beds.

The British soldier gave a sudden, strong, unexpected jerk. Once again, his leg popped free from Basil's grip.

"Hold him steady, now!" barked the doctor.

Basil complied. The physician quickly continued to probe the muscle of the man's thigh with a strange, silver-colored instrument. Every time he moved the device, the young man wailed louder.

"Martha! Bring that basin over here! And those extra bandages! Now!" Elizabeth lay across the man's chest, using her body weight to restrain his arms. She quickly wiped her hair away from her face. The coating of blood on her hand colored her forehead with a dark streak of crimson. She was growing weary from holding the man, and she was losing her patience with the pitifully inept surgeon.

Elizabeth spoke bitingly. "What else do you need, Doctor?"

The surgeon growled in disgust and tossed the metal probe into a blood-stained bowl. He exhaled, and then grumbled, "Get me my saw."

"Your saw?" Elizabeth exclaimed. "Not again, Dr. Peterson! His wound does not even appear to be that deep!"

Elizabeth's challenging of his decision greatly displeased him.

"Mrs. Billingsley, I cannot find the lead. It is lodged behind the bone. There are other men ... more seriously wounded men ... who require my attention. We must remove this leg and move on to the next patient."

"I will find the musket ball," Elizabeth declared.

"What?" exclaimed the surgeon.

"I said that I will find the ball. You may go and see to another patient."

"You most certainly will not! This is my patient, and I am responsible for his care!"

Elizabeth placed both fists on her hips. "And this is my house! This is my table upon which this poor man lies. Those are my sheets and towels and napkins that are soaked in his blood!" She growled, "At least let me try!"

The surgeon wiped his hands on a towel and tossed it onto the wounded man's chest. "As you wish, Mrs. Billingsley. I shall return in a short while, after you have failed in your foolish endeavor, and finish this job." He spun on his heels and stomped across the room.

Basil, still clutching the man's leg, stared at his mother with a mixture of disbelief and admiration. "What now, Mother?"

Elizabeth turned and examined the man's wound. "Basil, go and fetch the two large candelabras from upstairs, along with that tall side table from my bedchamber. I want as much light as I can get."

"Yes, Mother."

"And find us two helpers from somewhere. I need grown men who can help hold this fellow down."

"Yes, Mother."

"And tell Martha to bring that jug of rum from the pantry."

"Yes, Mother." Basil stood and stared at his mother, waiting for her next command.

Elizabeth shot an irritated glance at her son. "Well, what are you waiting for?"

"I thought you were going to say something else, Mother!"

"Off with you, boy! And quickly!"

Basil chuckled at his mother, quickly darted across the dining room, and then bounded up the staircase.

〜

One Hour Later

"I SIMPLY CANNOT BELIEVE IT, Mother. You did it!" Basil shook his head in admiration. He stared at the huge chunk of bloody lead in his hand. It was a flattened round ball, freshly retrieved from the soldier's thigh.

Basil, Elizabeth, and Martha were sitting on the back porch, resting their aching backs and weary heads against the cool brick wall. Little Anna slept peacefully in Martha's lap. All of the family members were exhausted from almost three hours of non-stop care of wounded British soldiers. Since the fighting had moved further west, there had been something of a lull in the arrival of the wounded. They took advantage of the slow-down as an opportunity for a brief rest break.

"You saved that man's leg, Mother," Martha exclaimed, snuggling tightly against her mother's arm. "I am so very proud of you."

Another rumble of nearby cannons caused the ground beneath the house to tremble. Leaves fell from some of the trees in the yard. A large plank suddenly dislodged and fell from the side of the barn.

Elizabeth shook her head in disgust. "A lot of good it will do him. He, and countless other boys, will surely die either on this horrible battlefield ... or on another."

Basil grunted spitefully. "Do not feel too much pity for them, Mother. Remember, they are our enemies. You have sons out there where those cannon balls are falling."

A tear welled in Elizabeth's eye. "As well I know, Basil. I have thought of nothing but James and John and Samuel since this ghastly fighting began. I pray that they are all safe."

"And Walter, too!" added Martha. "We must pray that he is safe, wherever he might be."

Basil shook his head slowly. He stared blankly into the thick woods behind their home. "I fear that Walter is likely on one of those death ships in Charlestown harbor."

"God forbid!" exclaimed Elizabeth. "I cannot bear the thought of it all!" She began to sob.

"I am sorry, Mother. I did not mean you make you cry." He reached for her hand and took it in his.

She squeezed his hand gently. "You did not make me cry, Basil. It is this horrible, terrible, frustrating war. I just want it to be done and for all my sons to come home."

The back door suddenly opened and a boot heel scraped across the rough wood floor at the far end of the porch. Dr. Peterson, the arrogant British surgeon, stood inside the threshold of the back door. He was wiping his bloody hands with a wet cloth. He had long-since shed his wool topcoat. His previously spotless white linen weskit and breeches were covered with blood stains.

"Please pardon the interruption, but we have a wagon out front, Mrs. Billingsley ... full of wounded. I require your assistance forthwith."

"Yes, Dr. Peterson. We will be right along."

The doctor nodded respectfully and then turned and marched back into the house. Just as the door closed behind him, Oliver came running from behind the barn.

"Basil! Basil! You must come and see!"

"Come and see what, Oliver?"

"Oliver Denkins! Where on earth have you been?" Elizabeth demanded.

"I was up in the loft, watching the battle off to the west. They've moved on a bit now. There are a powerful lot of men laying all over the ground in Mr. Sutton's field ... along that fence that runs near the road."

"Redcoats?" asked Basil.

"A few, but not many. Mostly other men in ordinary clothes."

Basil glanced quickly at his mother. "Militia!" he hissed.

"Is anyone tending to them?" she asked Oliver. "Are there medics or surgeons?"

"No, ma'am. They are all just lying there. I did not see any anything moving in the field."

Elizabeth nodded to her son. "Go, Basil, and take a look. Help anyone that you can. Take Oliver with you. But, stay out of sight of the Redcoats!"

"Yes, Mother. C'mon, Oliver!"

Basil rose to his feet and both boys sprinted into the tree-line that led toward the battlefield.

THE TWO BOYS knelt beside another fallen Patriot militiaman near the wooden fence. Basil checked for breathing, but there was none. Like all of the others that they had already examined, the poor man was dead.

"Basil, this is horrible!" wailed Oliver. "I have never seen anything like it. No one is alive!" Swollen teardrops inched down both of his dirt-stained cheeks.

"We have to keep looking, Oliver. There is still hope." He nodded toward the trees that were fifty yards to their west. "Let's check those woods."

Oliver nodded. Both boys darted toward the trees. They heard the rumble of cannons from behind them and listened to the terrifying howl of the cannon balls as they soared over their heads. The boys dropped to the ground and covered their heads. Moments later the balls exploded against the ground far to the west.

"Was that very close?" Oliver asked with a trembling voice.

Basil shook his head. "No, Oliver. I think it was very far off. We are safe, I think ... unless the Patriots break through the lines and push the British back. Let us be quick, and see if we can help anyone."

The boys rose and pushed onward toward the woods. As they neared the trees, they saw that the timber had been decimated by cannon fire. Many of the tree trunks were shattered by explosions. Broken limbs, shards of wood, and fallen timbers lay haphazardly upon the ground.

"I see wounded men!" Basil exclaimed, pointing to the right.

They ran in the direction of several fallen soldiers. Suddenly, Oliver stopped running and began screaming in a piercing, frantic voice. He instantly dropped to his hands and knees. His back and chest heaved as he threw up his dinner onto the leaf-strewn ground. Basil fought the urge to vomit, as well. Nearby lay a man who had received the full force of a cannon ball. His body had been decimated by the explosion.

Somehow, Basil managed to keep his wits about him. He turned away from the ghastly sight of the dismembered man and looked at another poor fellow who lay sprawled, face-down, against the base of a tree. Basil gripped the man's shoulder and flipped him onto his back. The wounded man gave a slight groan.

"This one is alive, Oliver! He is alive! Come and help me!"

Oliver climbed onto unsteady feet and stumbled toward

Basil. He knelt down on the other side of the motionless man.

"Wha ... what's wrong with him?" Oliver stammered.

Basil pointed to his legs. His breeches were torn and bloody. "It looks like he has some metal pieces in his legs." He leaned over and listened to the fellow's heart. "His heartbeat and breathing are strong. I think he will be all right. His head is a bit bloody, though."

Basil reached up and brushed the fellow's long, stringy hair away from his blood-crusted forehead. He gave a sudden gasp, and then exclaimed, "Oh, God! Oh, God! Oh, thank you, God!" Tears began to flow down his cheeks.

Oliver gripped Basil's arm. "What is it, Basil? What is wrong?"

Basil locked eyes with the young boy. His face was covered with tears, but a huge smile consumed his entire face. "Oliver, nothing is wrong! This is my brother! This is Walter ... the one who was in prison in South Carolina! He is alive!"

12

EVACUATION

"How can he be here?" Oliver demanded. "It makes no sense!"

"I do not know. But, here he lies ... in the flesh."

Basil checked his brother's breathing once again. The sounds in his lungs remained strong. He was unconscious, but did not appear to be critically wounded.

"I am worried about that injury to his head," Basil mumbled. "We should be able to get the metal pieces out of his legs easily enough. But, it looks like he slammed his skull pretty hard against this tree."

Oliver frowned. "What are we going to do with him? He needs to see a doctor, but we cannot take him back to our house. The British are everywhere in town."

"Somehow, we have to get him to the Continentals. We can try their encampment first."

"How will we get him there?" Oliver challenged. "It is over two miles away."

He pointed toward the south. "We can make a litter and drag him through the woods. It's only about a half-mile to the big buffalo trail. The wagon that we hid in the woods is not far. We can load him in the rig and take him to the American surgeons."

"What about the horses? They are back in the barn," Oliver observed.

Basil nodded. "If you will sit with Walter when we reach the wagon, I will sneak into the barn and get the team of horses. We can get him to the Patriot encampment within the hour."

Oliver nodded excitedly. "It is a good plan, Basil."

IT TOOK LONGER than the boys anticipated to move the wounded Walter Billingsley. They rigged a litter out of sapling poles and the wool coats of two fallen British soldiers. Despite his emaciated state and loss of weight during captivity, Walter was still a heavy load for them to drag. The boys were exhausted when, over an hour later, they reached the wagon in its place of concealment deep in the woods.

The boys struggled to load Walter in the back of the wagon, but eventually succeeded in completing the difficult task.

"All right, Oliver ... you remain here and rest whilst I go and fetch the horses."

"I'm mighty thirsty," Oliver groaned.

Basil pointed to his right. "There is a spring about forty yards up this path. Take two of the canteens from beneath the wagon seat. Drink what you want at the spring, and then fill both of them. Try to get some water into Walter. Hopefully, he will be able to swallow. Then, wait for me to return.

Stay with the wagon. Remain out of sight and keep quiet. I will get back as quickly as I can."

"Yes, Basil." Oliver trembled slightly with fear.

A cannon exploded in the distance. Oliver instinctively dipped his head. A frown of worry filled his face.

Basil reassured him, "Everything will be all right, Ollie. There are no British near here. They are several miles to the west. You will be safe. I promise." Basil reached for the lad and pulled him close. He hugged him tightly.

"I will be waiting for you, right here at the wagon," Oliver declared.

Basil grinned, knocked Oliver's black cocked hat off of his head, and tousled his already-messy hair. Then, quick as a flash, he jumped from the wagon bed and took off running down the trail toward home.

Late Afternoon – Near the American Encampment

AT LONG LAST, the rumble of cannons had stopped. There was no more shooting, no more drums, and no more screaming voices echoing across the fields and valleys of Guilford County. Finally, the Battle of Guilford Courthouse was over.

Basil was completely exhausted. Though he was worried about his mother and sister, all of his attention was focused on his brother, Walter. He simply had to get him to the doctors at the Patriot encampment. He snapped the reins and clucked at his team of horses, urging the animals onward along the rutted, dusty road. The strong beasts leaned forward and tugged the heavy wagon up a rather steep hill.

"Less than a mile to go!" Basil whispered to himself.

Getting Walter to the soldier camp had been a far more difficult task than Basil had anticipated. Securing a team of horses from the Billingsley barn had been extremely difficult. There were entirely too many British soldiers milling and lingering about the town. The fact that his home was serving as a makeshift British hospital seemed to attract the enemy soldiers in great numbers. It had taken Basil almost an hour to sneak the two huge animals, one at a time, through the rear door of the barn.

Once he had the horses secured and hooked up to the wagon, he discovered that maneuvering the rig through the woods was more difficult that it had been only days before. The winding trail through the forest was extremely narrow and strewn with limbs from a recent spring storm. Some of those limbs were quite large. On multiple occasions, both Basil and Oliver had been forced to climb down from the wagon and clear debris from their path in order to reach the westward road that led to the camp.

Basil stared southward down the wagon road and shook his head, disgusted. He had expected it to take less than an hour to get Walter to the army hospital. But, it had been almost four hours since he had discovered his long-lost brother on the battlefield near Guilford Courthouse. Basil worried nervously for his wounded sibling. He uttered a silent prayer for Walter's well-being.

Basil glanced over his shoulder at his passengers, both of whom lay silently in the back of the wagon. Walter's visible wounds had stopped bleeding, but he had still not regained consciousness. Little Oliver slept soundly, nestled against Walter's side. The lad snored lightly, uttering a raspy click that sounded almost like the purring of a cat. Basil smiled ever-so-slightly. He was amazed at how Oliver was able to sleep, even in the hard, rough bed of the jostling wagon.

Minutes later, the wagon topped the hill and Walter spied the American encampment. The place was a beehive of activity. Hundreds of soldiers were taking down tents, dousing fires, and loading wagons. Basil spied several formations of soldiers marching westward in the direction of the Quaker villages.

The road in front of Basil remained blocked by a checkpoint about one hundred yards outside the camp. A single, lonely militiaman manned the post. He stepped reluctantly into the road in front of Basil's wagon and raised his French Charleville musket across his chest.

"Halt!" he exclaimed. "No one is allowed into the camp."

Basil exhaled, frustrated. "Mister, I do not have time for this. I have a wounded militiaman in my wagon, and I need to get him to the hospital now!"

The soldier marched toward the wagon to investigate. He glanced over the sideboards at the two bodies in the bed of the wagon.

"What's wrong with the little one?" the soldier asked, curious.

"Nothing. He is just sleeping."

The soldier stared at Walter. Basil tapped his foot nervously against the footboard. He was growing impatient.

"What is his regiment?" inquired the soldier.

"I do not know ... but he is the brother of Captain James Billingsley."

The militiaman's left eyebrow raised high. "Of the Rowan County Regiment?"

Basil nodded.

"How do you know that?"

"Because he's my brother, too."

Both of the soldier's eyebrows raised in surprise. "Indeed? Do you know where Captain Billingsley's company is bivouacked?"

"Yes, sir. I have been there before."

"Good. Go on through, then. But you are not going to find any doctors or hospital tents here. They've moved on to the west ... to the Troublesome Iron Works. They are collecting casualties there."

"Why so far?" asked Basil.

"Because we lost the battle today. The British took the ground. We killed many of Cornwallis' soldiers, but those wretched Redcoats drove us from the field."

Basil's heart sank. He nodded and tipped the brim of his cocked hat. "Thank you for letting us into the camp, sir."

The soldier smiled thinly and nodded. He quickly tilted his head in the direction of the camp. "You are most welcome. Now, go and find your brother. I am quite certain that he will be glad to see you ... and this wagon. We are running short on transportation for our wounded and our supplies."

Basil snapped the reins and guided his team of horses through the chaos of the camp.

A sleepy voice called from the back of the wagon. "Where are we, Basil?"

"We are at the camp. We should be with James and the Rowan County boys here in just a bit."

Basil heard leather scraping against the poplar floorboards in the wagon. Oliver slowly climbed over the seat and took his place beside Basil.

"Did you have a nice nap?" the older boy teased.

"Quite nice, thank you." He stretched and rubbed his stiff, aching shoulder. He quipped, "Now, I would really like some tea and biscuits, please."

"Hopefully, we can find some food here in the camp."

Minutes later Basil caught sight of his older brother, James. The captain was busy directing his men to load their supplies into a small hand-pulled cart. When the elder Billingsley saw Basil and Oliver, his eyes opened wide. He darted quickly toward the wagon.

"Basil! Oliver! What, in Heaven's Name, are you boys doing here? What is wrong? Has something happened to Mother?" His voice sounded almost frantic.

Basil and Oliver climbed down from the wagon seat. James grabbed them both and surrounded them with a huge bear-hug.

Basil replied, "No, James. Mother is fine. The British are all in Guilford Courthouse. Hundreds of them. They actually set up a hospital in our house. The place is crawling with Redcoats, but Mother is fine. She's giving the British surgeons all kinds of grief."

James grinned broadly. "Well, Cornwallis should be pulling out of there soon. Our scouts say they are already moving toward the southeast. They took the field, but at a very high price. I suspect they will be reeling from their losses for quite some time. But, Basil, you did not answer my question. Why are you here?"

"Mother sent Oliver and me out to check the wounded in Sutton's field after the British were over the hill. No one seemed to be caring for the American soldiers. We only found one man alive. He is someone you know." Basil nodded toward the wagon.

James strode toward the rig and glanced over the side. His mouth hung open in disbelief.

Oliver chirped, "It's your brother, Walter!"

"I know it is Walter, young man. But, how did he come to

be in the battle today? He is supposed to be in a British prison in South Carolina!"

Basil shrugged. "I have no idea. But here he is. And he's hurt, James. His legs are bloody, but will be all right, I think. But he took a strong blow to the head. He has not been awake since we found him."

"How long ago was that?"

"Just after dinner time. It's been several hours."

James grimaced. "He needs to see one of our surgeons immediately, but they are all several miles to the west."

"I know. At the iron works," responded Basil. "The guard at the checkpoint told us."

James thought for a moment. "You boys are going to have to come with us. We need the wagon, anyhow. We have four other wounded men. We were afraid that we might have to leave them behind. But, now we can load them in your wagon and get them to the surgeons, as well."

Basil nodded. "We can fill up any extra space with supplies."

"Indeed," James affirmed. "Let us make haste. We must get our brother to the field hospital, and quickly!"

13

FAMILY REUNION

Three Days Later

Walter Billingsley opened his eyes. He was staring at a low ceiling. He heard the dull rumble of distant thunder, and the high-pitched dripping of water as it landed in buckets and puddles. He raised up on his left elbow and looked around. The floor beside him was littered with wounded men. Most appeared to be soldiers of the militia. There were a handful of Continentals, as well. On the far side of the room he spied several red coats. They were the enemy wounded, isolated from the Patriots and under guard.

A voice shouted from across the room, "Doctor Edmonds, that fellow with the head injury is awake!"

An older gentleman appeared at Walter's side almost immediately. "Ah! Walter! Awake at last! We feared that you may have slipped into a permanent slumber."

Walter was confused. He had never seen this man before.

"Sir ... how do you know my name?"

"Your brothers told me. I am Dr. Enoch Edmonds, surgeon in charge of this ward."

"My brothers?" Walter exclaimed. The shout sent a wave of pain through his head.

"I suggest that you remain calm, Walter. You have had a serious blow to the top of your head."

Walter nodded. "Which of my brothers are here?"

The doctor pointed across the room. "Samuel is over there in the far corner. He is sleeping soundly. The poor lad took some iron fragments in his back. From the cannon fire, you know."

"Will he live?"

"Samuel will be just fine. His wounds were mostly superficial. Lots of blood, but not particularly deep. The fragments were quite easy to remove. He'll be on his way home in a couple of days."

The doctor pulled the blanket off of Walter's legs. "You took some of the same in your legs, I am afraid. I got most of it out. There are a couple of pieces in the muscle of your lower left leg that were a bit too deep. But, your body should close them off with time. Everything looks pink and clean. There is no bloody pus or foul smell."

"My head hurts badly," Walter complained.

"As well it should. It looks like you tried to use it to chop down a tree. And it appears like you attempted to sand that tree smooth with your face," he teased. "But, the cuts and scrapes will heal soon enough. The knot on the top of your head has gone down quite a bit. You may keep a headache for quite some time, but you're young and strong. You will heal quickly. Count your blessings, boy. None of your innards were hurt. Heart, lungs, guts, and liver are all untouched. There's many a man inside this building who cannot claim the same."

"How long have I been sleeping?" asked Walter, scanning at his surroundings.

"Almost three days. Your body needed the rest. We are bivouacked at the Troublesome Iron Works, about fifteen miles west of the battlefield. General Greene ordered us to remain here long enough to care for our wounded and get resupplied."

Walter nodded his understanding. "You said that I have brothers here ... as in more than one. Are any of the others besides Samuel nearby?"

"James is at his company's campsite. I sent an orderly for him. He should be here soon. I think the Rowan County boys can survive for a little while without their captain." He smiled warmly.

∿

One Hour Later

A SMILING CAPTAIN JAMES BILLINGSLEY came bursting through the door of the hospital. He sprinted to Walter's mat.

"Walter! You hard-headed little cuss! How are you? When can you go home?"

"I have a raging headache, but the surgeon says I'll live. He said that I might be able to go home tomorrow or the day after." Walter immediately unleashed a barrage of questions. "How is mother? How are our brothers and sisters? Did the British get into the town? Did our house suffer any harm?"

James knelt down and hugged his brother gently. "Everyone is just fine. John is with his company. Samuel is asleep in the corner. He is wounded, but doing well."

Walter nodded. "Dr. Edmonds told me about Samuel."

James continued, "I checked on Mother, Martha, and Anna yesterday. Mother is worried sick about you, of course. The British occupied Guilford, took over the house and used it for a hospital for two days, but they eventually left and headed east. Mother is slowly but surely returning everything to its normal place. She is angry that they ruined all of her sheets and linens, but she will get over it ... someday." He chuckled lightly and a smile filled his face. "She has been cleaning and scrubbing for three days now, working desperately to rid the house of any evidence of British invasion."

Walter appeared confused. "Who is Anna?"

James laughed. "That's right! You have never met her, before! Or her brother, Oliver. They are a couple of orphans that mother has taken in. Basil caught them stealing chickens. They were living in a cave in the woods. They somehow managed to wander up here last winter all the way from Georgia. Of course, Mother could not simply leave them on their own out in the woods. So, she took them in. Martha is quite smitten with the little girl." He smiled broadly. "It looks like we will be raising another couple of little ones. They're not Billingsleys, but close enough, I suppose."

Walter's mind reeled. He could scarcely imagine orphans ... strangers ... sleeping in his home.

"What about Basil? How is he? Is he safe?" Walter demanded.

James nodded enthusiastically. "He will be right along. He and Oliver just hauled a wagon-load of supplies into camp from New Market. I sent a runner over to fetch him when I got word that you were awake. He should be here soon. I imagine the rain has slowed them down a bit."

Tears formed in the corners of Walter's eyes. Despite all

of the fighting and teasing of childhood, it was Basil that he had missed the most. They had been inseparable in their youth. They had grown up sleeping in the same room. They had often lain awake late into the night, sharing stories and laughing together. They did all of their daily chores together. They ate every meal together. Basil was "Little Brother," to him. It was a nickname that had once been intended to tease, but had become over time a term of endearment.

It was James' turn to ask some questions. "The last we heard, you were being held at Camden, and likely headed for a prison ship in the harbor at Charlestown. What happened? How did you get away, and how on earth did you wind up in this battle?"

Walter frowned. "The story is much too long to tell, James, in this current circumstance. Perhaps, once we have all returned home and this war is done, I can tell all of you at once."

"All right, Walter. If that is what you wish." James paused. "Your war is over, by the way."

"Whatever do you mean?" Walter challenged him.

"I have already secured your discharge from General Butler. You will be going straightway home as soon as the doctors release you. And you will not be fighting, anymore, in this confounded war. I believe that you have been through enough already."

"More than you can imagine, Jamie ... more than you can imagine." Walters voice trailed off into silence.

"There is something else you need to know, Walter," James declared.

"What?"

"It was Basil who actually found you wounded on the battlefield. He and Oliver carried you overland to the wagon and then brought you all the way here to Troublesome Iron Works." James smiled proudly.

"Little Brother saved my life?" Walter asked in disbelief.

"He did, indeed."

Walter choked back an overwhelming urge to cry out loud.

At the Supply Tent

BASIL AND OLIVER only had two more sacks of corn left to unload. They were glad. It had been a long, wet, and miserable day hauling freight in the pouring-down rain. Both boys were anxious to find some dry clothes, a mug of hot tea, and a warm bed.

A messenger suddenly burst through the open door of the tent. "Is there a Basil Billingsley here?"

Basil waved at the man. "I am he. Why do you ask?"

The winded fellow took a deep breath. "Cap'n Billingsley says you need to get over to the hospital, and quickly so. Your brother is awake!"

Basil glanced in disbelief at Oliver, then spun and darted toward the door. Oliver followed, barely a step behind him. Basil forgot all about the rain. He did not care that he was already soaked to the bone and freezing cold. He simply had to see his big brother! He ran full-speed, ignoring the huge puddles of mud that filled the narrow road to the stone building that served as the camp hospital.

BASIL APPEARED UNANNOUNCED beside Walter's cot. He was

wearing a rain-soaked hunting frock and a black felt floppy hat. He quickly removed the hat, tossed it to the ground, and knelt down on the ground beside his wounded brother. He was smiling from ear to ear. He took Walter's hand in his own.

"Walter! I am so glad that you are awake! I have worried myself sick over you! How are you feeling?"

Walter squinted and stared as his younger brother. He barely recognized the young man kneeling beside him. Basil's long hair was pulled back into a perfect queue. His face looked more angular. His "baby fat" was gone from his cheeks and chin. Basil seemed older. Walter even spied a stubble of whiskers on his rain-soaked face.

"I am better now, Basil." He glanced proudly at James. "And I hear that I have you to thank for it."

Basil's face flushed red. "It wasn't just me. Oliver helped. Allow me introduce you." He grabbed Oliver by the arm and pulled him toward the mat. "Walter, this is Oliver Denkins. He lives with us now, along with his little sister, Anna. They have been a big help to Mother over this past year. Oliver, this is my big brother and best friend, Walter."

Oliver mumbled, "I am pleased to finally meet you, Walter."

"Likewise, Oliver. I am most grateful to you for helping get me off of the battlefield. I also heard that you helped take care of me. I owe you a great debt."

Oliver grinned with pride.

Basil grinned. "We have us a new little brother at our house now, Walter. I think I like it."

A tear flowed down Walter's cheek. He smiled. "I suppose all of us Billingsley boys needed another little brother. You have definitely outgrown the title."

Basil grinned broadly and squeezed his brother's hand.

He glanced over his shoulder and asked loudly, "When can I take him home, Doc?"

Dr. Edmonds wandered over from the far side of the room. "We can see how things are going in the morning. If Walter is improved, and if the weather is better, perhaps you can remove him after dinner tomorrow. But, I am not making any promises. It all depends upon his amount of improvement between now and then."

Basil nodded. "I understand." He turned and faced his wounded brother. "Are you hungry, Walter? Do you need anything? Anything, at all?"

His big brother nodded. "I am famished, now that you mention it. No one in this place has offered me a bite to eat."

Basil glanced at the doctor. "What about it, Doc? Can we feed him?"

Dr. Edmonds knitted his brow. "Liquids only for now. Perhaps some broth or soup."

"I think I can come up with some chicken soup, even if I have to strangle one of the birds, myself." Basil grinned broadly and stood upright. "Walter, grant me leave to go and change into some dry clothes. Then, I will be back in a bit with some hot soup. We have many stories to tell, and much reacquainting to do."

"That sounds wonderful, Basil," Walter declared. Tears flowed freely down his cheeks.

"Can I come back with you, too?" Oliver asked excitedly. "I want to know more about Walter."

Basil slapped the waterlogged brim of the boy's cocked hat. "Of course, you can!" He paused, glanced down at a smiling Walter, and then added two beautiful, loving words ... "Little Brother."

THE REAL BASIL BILLINGSLEY

Though this story is entirely fictional, Basil was a real person, and many of the elements in the story were based upon actual events. Basil was the youngest son of James and Elizabeth Crabtree Billingsley. His father was, indeed, hanged by Tories near the Billingsley home in early 1776. All of his older brothers, except for Henry, left behind records of their military service during the American Revolution.

Tragically, little is known about Basil. Family records show that he was born in 1764 in Baltimore, Maryland. His family lived there until they migrated to North Carolina in the late 1760's. He filed for a plot of land in nearby Rowan County in 1784, around the age of twenty. After that, the records are difficult to decipher. His older brother, Samuel, appears to have named his oldest son, Basil. Indeed, it was a Billingsley family name that stretched back for several generations. This duplication of names makes it difficult to track our Basil Billingsley through time.

So, in the end, we are left searching and wondering. We simply do not know what happened to Basil Billingsley, son of James and Elizabeth. Perhaps, he died at a young age. We simply cannot discern the truth based upon the limited records.

Still, even though we do not know what happened to the real Basil Billingsley, we do know that he was the "Little Brother" to all of the other Billingsley boys. It was a pleasure to make him the hero of this story.

REVOLUTIONARY WAR / COLONIAL GLOSSARY
SOME STRANGE WORDS YOU MAY ENCOUNTER

Barracks – A form of housing or dormitory for soldiers. Their primary function was for sleeping. Often dozens of men were housed in these large buildings.

Bayonet – The sharp knife-like instrument that connects to the end of a military musket. It was used most often in hand-to-hand fighting.

Bedchamber – The common 18th century word for bedroom.

Blockhouse – The corner structure that was usually included into the structure of the walls of a fort.

Breeches – These were the pants of the colonial period. They were secured with buttons and baggy in the seat. The pants reached just below the knee. Men typically wore long socks that covered their lower leg and extended up over the knee.

Brown Bess Musket – This is the name given to the British Army's military musket. They were mass-produced, smooth-barreled flintlock weapons that fired a .75 caliber (¾ inch) round lead ball.

Bullet / Ball / Musket Ball – The round lead balls fired from 18th century weapons.

Bullet Mold – Sized steel molds used to make rifle and musket projectiles. Melted lead was poured into these molds and allowed to cool, thus producing balls perfectly sized for weapons of the period.

Cannon – The artillery of Revolutionary War. These giant guns loaded through the muzzle and fired either large steel balls or clusters of steel or lead known as **grapeshot.**

Canteen – A receptacle used by soldiers to carry their personal supply of water.

Cartridge – These were pre-rolled ammunition packs for muskets. Made from paper, each cartridge resembled a stubby cigar, and contained the proper amount of gunpowder and a single lead projectile. Soldiers tore the cartridges open with their teeth, poured the gunpowder down the barrel of their weapon, and then rammed the paper and musket ball down the barrel.

Cease-Fire – A temporary stoppage of fighting, usually giving officers of opposing armies the opportunity to talk to one another under parley.

Charleville Musket – A French army musket that was common during the period of the American Revolution. It was a smooth-barreled flintlock weapon that fired a .69 caliber round lead ball.

Compatriots – Soldiers who fight alongside one another.

Continental Army – Soldiers in the federal army of United States as authorized by the Continental Congress.

Crown – The shortened form of "**British Crown.**" It was a reference to the form of British government, which was a kingdom. The king or queen was the wearer of the "crown."

Dragoons – A special type of soldier in the British army.

They were "mounted infantry" who could either fight on horseback or on foot.

Earthworks – Piles of dirt, rock, and wood used as a barricade to protect soldiers from enemy gunfire. Soldiers often constructed these around their forts or around places that they were attacking.

Flintlock – The type of weapons, loaded through the muzzle, used during the American Revolution.

Frizzen – The part of a flintlock weapon that the flint strikes to make a spark and ignite the gunpowder.

Gallows – Structures used for the execution of criminals by hanging.

Guardhouse – The jail inside a military facility.

Gunpowder – Also called "**powder**," this was an explosive compound that was used to fire weapons. Many men on the frontier carried their powder in hollowed out horns from bulls called, "**powder horns.**"

His Majesty – The proper, formal reference to the King of England. A queen is called, "Her Majesty."

Huzzah – A joyful shout, and the early form of the modern words "hoorah" and "hooray."

Indentured Servitude – This was a form of "voluntary slavery" in which poor people signed over their freedom to wealthy people for a set period of time. In return for their years of servitude they earned something such as passage by ship to America, the learning of a work trade, or shelter and food.

Indian – A traditional term used to refer to Native Americans. The term arose out of the confusion of early explorers. When they arrived in the Americas they thought that they had reached the east coast of India. Therefore, they referred to the native peoples as "Indians." The name "stuck" and became a word of common use in the United States.

Injun – The slang word for "Indian," or Native American.

Lead – The soft metal used to make projectiles for rifles and muskets. It is still used to make modern projectiles.

Leggings – Also known as "**Gaiters**," these were protective garments for the lower legs. They were often made of wool, canvas, cotton, or animal skins. They were secured with buttons or straps and served to protect and insulate the exposed lower leg between the breeches and shoes.

Litter – A makeshift vehicle used to transport sick or wounded soldiers. Similar to a modern stretcher, it was often made of cloth or animal skins suspended between two poles. It could be carried by people on foot or dragged behind a horse.

Long Knives – Recorded also as **Big Knives**, this was the name given by the local Native Americans to the Virginia Army under Col. George Rogers Clark.

Loyalist – A citizen of the American colonies loyal to King George III and Great Britain.

Militia – Local county and state military units. Most served locally. There were both Patriot and Loyalist militia units during the war. French militia units served with either the British or American forces.

Moccasins – Typical lightweight footwear of the Eastern Woodland Indians. Made from animal hides, these shoes often had a thread that was pulled through the leather on top that caused it to have its distinguishing "pucker."

Muster – The official forming of local militia units for mobilization in the war.

Necessary House – This was the common name for an outhouse or outdoor toilet in the 18th Century.

Oath of Allegiance – This was a custom in the 1700's. Men would "swear their oath" to a nation, state, or king as a demonstration of their loyalty. Men who swore such oaths usually signed their names on official documents. In the Revolutionary War this was a demonstration of Patriotic Service either to England or to the United States.

Palisades – Walls made from upright stakes or tree trunks that were often pointed on top. They were built for defense, such as in the walls of primitive forts.

Parley – Formal negotiations between opposing armies.

Patriots – People in American who were in favor of separation from England and the formation of a separate country.

Patrol – A military tactic which involved sending soldiers out into the countryside to scout for any presence of the enemy.

Queue – Pronounced "kew." This is the word for a man's ponytail. Men in Colonial times wore their hair long. They would often tie it in the back or braid it into a queue.

Redcoats – The derogatory name that Patriots called British soldiers.

Runner – Before the development of modern technology, messages had to be carried "on foot." Men or boys who delivered messages between a commander and the army were simply called "runners."

Sentry – A soldier who stands guard at a military encampment or facility, or along a roadway. Armies placed sentries on duty any time they wanted to keep an eye out for enemy soldiers or suspicious activity.

Spectacles – The old name for eyeglasses.

Shooting Pouch – A leather bag worn by frontiersmen. They carried their ammunition and tools for taking care of their musket or rifle in the pouch.

Siege – A military tactic in which an army surrounds another army, usually confined in a town or fort. Once the enemy army is contained, the army laying siege bombards them with fire until the army under siege calls for a surrender.

Station – Another name for a frontier fort.

Surgeon – A military doctor. The practice of medicine was quite different during the Colonial period. There were not many medical schools or universities. Many doctors learned "on the job" from other doctors. Military surgeons spent most of their time treating battle wounds and the various diseases that afflicted their armies.

Surrender – The formal, official end of a military conflict when one army acknowledges that the other is victor. Surrender often has certain terms to which both parties in the negotiation must agree.

Tankard – A large, cylindrical drinking cup with a single handle. Often made of wood, pewter, brass, or tin.

Tomahawk – A bladed weapon that resembled an axe or hatchet. This useful tool was used both in combat as well as in camp life.

Tory / Tories – Another name for Loyalists.

Wax Seal – People usually sealed their private letters with a melted blob of hot wax and then pressed a piece of metal into the wax to make an impression or "seal." This was a way to ensure that private letters were not opened until they reached their destination.

Weskit – Also known as a **waistcoat**, this was the vest worn over the top of a man's shirt and under a man's coat. It would sometimes be worn without the outer overcoat. It was a more formal outer garment.

A MESSAGE FROM THE AUTHOR

Thank You For Reading My Story!

I hope that you enjoyed my work of fiction. It was a pleasure preparing and writing it for you. I am just a simple "part-time" author, and I am humbled that you chose to read my book.

I would like to ask you to help me spread the word about my historical fiction books for kids. You can actually help me in a number of ways!

•**Tell your friends!** Word of mouth is always the best! Just tell them how much you enjoyed my story.

•**Mention my books on Facebook or in other social media.** I know lots of students use social media these days. Please mention me, or maybe even post a picture of you reading one of my books! Be sure to go to my Author Page and give me a "Like."

•**Get your parents to write a review for me on Amazon.com.** Reviews are so very important. They help other readers discover good books. Tell your parents what you thought about the book and ask them to put your words into the review.

•**Connect with me and like my author page on Facebook @cockedhatpublishing, and follow me on Twitter @GeoffBaggett.**

•**Tell your teachers about me!** I have a unique and interesting Revolutionary War presentation available for elementary and middle school classes. I actually bring a trunk full of items from the American Revolution and provide a "hands-on" experience for students. I even dress up couple of volunteers in replica Revolutionary War militia uniforms! I am a professional speaker and living historian, and I absolutely love to travel and visit in schools. Get your teachers to contact me through my web site, geoffbaggett.com, or through my Facebook author page, to arrange an event.

Thanks again! And remember to tell all of your friends about the *Patriot Kids of the American Revolution Series*!

Geoff Baggett

ABOUT THE AUTHOR

Geoff Baggett is a historical researcher and author with a passion for all things Revolutionary War. He is an active member of the Sons of the American Revolution and the Descendants of Washington's Army at Valley Forge.

Geoff has discovered over twenty American Patriot ancestors in his family tree. He is an avid living historian, appearing regularly in period clothing and uniforms in classrooms, reenactments, and other commemorative events. He lives with his family on a quiet little place in the country in rural western Kentucky.

Made in the USA
Monee, IL
23 November 2020